Spilling the Beans

Spilling the Beans

by Beth Cruise

BOXTREE

First published in the UK 1995 by BOXTREE LIMITED
Broadwall House, 21 Broadwall, London SE1 9PL

First published in the United States 1994 by Aladdin Books, Macmillan
Publishing Company, 866 Third Avenue, New York, NY10022

10 9 8 7 6 5 4 3 2 1

Printed and bound in Great Britain by Cox & Wyman, Reading, Berkshire

A catalogue record for this book is available from the British Library

ISBN 0 7522 0660 5

To Peter Engel

1

Megan Jones stalked into the Max, her dark eyes flashing with anger. She stopped at the door and looked around the favorite hangout of everyone at Bayside High. It was packed, as usual, but she finally spotted some familiar faces. Vicki Needleman, her best friend, was sitting at a table with Weasel Wyzell and Scott Ericson.

Just then, Vicki saw Megan and waved to her, flipping her blond hair over her shoulder.

Vicki was a great friend—when she wasn't talking about her sinuses. And Scott was turning out to be a pretty nice guy. When he first started at Bayside a couple of months earlier, it had seemed like he was a real troublemaker. But Scott was the kind of guy who learned from his mistakes, and Megan was beginning to feel like she could depend on him.

She walked up to the table, ready to vent her anger.

"Boys! Forget it. I'm never talking to another boy as long as I live!" Megan slammed her books down on the table.

"Hey, watch it!" Weasel squeaked. "You almost stuck your book in the middle of my cheese fries!" He put his arm protectively around his plate, which was covered with a revolting mass of melted cheese food product, fried potato, and ketchup.

"I'm sorry, Weasel," Megan apologized. "I didn't mean to yell at you." She didn't want to hurt Weasel's feelings. Sure, he was annoying, he dressed like a nerd, and in times of stress he asked her to marry him—but he was always there when she needed him, too.

"What happened, Megan?" Vicki asked, her blue eyes wide with curiosity. "Didn't your date with Jeffrey work out?"

Megan sighed and sat down. "It was horrible," she said. "I mean, he is so cute—"

"*Way* cute," Vicki interrupted. "We are talking maximum cuteness. That wavy hair . . . , those bulging soccer-player muscles . . . , that awesome tan . . ."

"*Vicki!*" Megan snapped. "It was *my* date!"

"Oh, right!" Vicki said. "Sorry. What went wrong?"

"He's a total doofus," Megan replied. "I mean, he doesn't care about school or learning or anything. I asked him what the last book he read was, and he said the *Sports Illustrated* swimsuit issue!"

"Yeah, I could have told you that," Scott said, leaning back in his chair. "Jeff is in my history class. He makes Arnold Schwarzenegger look like a major poet. The only words I ever hear him say are *ugh, cool,* and *not!*"

"I had to tutor him once," Weasel piped up. "He tried to put a computer disk into his CD player."

"That's totally impossible. No one could be that dumb!" Vicki said, giggling. "I don't believe it!"

"Believe it," Megan sighed, reaching over to Weasel's plate and dipping the least cheesy fry she could find into a puddle of ketchup. "This guy is pretty dopey. We had absolutely nothing to talk about. We just kind of stared at each other until I made up some story about having a book report to do, and he walked me home. I don't even think he's that cute anymore."

"But Megan! What about the big Halloween dance that's coming up?" Vicki asked.

"I don't know. I was hoping Jeffrey would ask me, but not anymore," Megan said. "I am totally sick of boys."

"But the dance is a really big deal!" Vicki cried. "We've got to have dates."

"Look, Vicki," Megan said, "I'd love to go to the dance. But if there's one special guy out there who's perfect for me, I haven't found him yet. And I'd rather stay home than spend time with someone I can't even talk to."

"I guess you're right," Vicki sighed. "I'm going to save myself for that one special guy, too. . . . Right, Scott?" She put her hand on Scott's arm and fluttered her eyelashes at him. She had gotten a crush on Scott when he started at Bayside, and even though she had pretty much given up on him by now, she still got moony about him every once in a while.

"Uh—hey, I kinda like being single," Scott said, sitting up suddenly. "I can't be tied to just one woman." *Unless that woman is Lindsay Warner,* he started to think; but then he stopped himself. True, Lindsay was one of the coolest and prettiest girls he had ever met. But she was stuck like glue to her boyfriend, Tommy DeLuca. And Scott had to admit, they made a great couple.

4

"Yeah! Scott's a free agent," Weasel put in. "Me and Scott are just a couple of studs on the loose. We're like Batman and Robin! Like Captain Kirk and Mr. Spock!"

"You mean, like Ernie and Bert?" Megan asked.

"Hey!" Weasel protested. He was about to complain, when something caught his eye. It was a red scarf around the neck of a dark, intense-looking girl. "Oh, no," Weasel whispered. "It's her!"

"Who's her?" Vicki asked, looking around the room. "Who are you looking at?"

"Weasel, are you in love again?" Megan asked.

"In love? Not this time," Weasel squeaked. "It's Manya. Over there." He gestured with his head.

Everyone looked.

"Don't look!" Weasel shrieked.

Scott, Vicki, and Megan all snapped their heads back around to stare at their friend.

"Uh—Weasel?" Scott said. "You want to tell us what's going on with this girl?"

"She's in the computer class that I'm helping to teach," Weasel whispered, leaning forward. "She's from Russia."

"And?" Scott whispered back.

"And someone said her father was in the KGB," Weasel continued.

5

"What *is* the KGB?" Vicki asked.

"It's a secret spy society. Kind of like the CIA and the FBI combined," Megan told her. "They used to keep tabs on people in the old Soviet Union."

"Oh." Vicki thought for a minute, then looked back at Weasel. "So?"

"*So?*" Weasel yelled. People at the next table turned and looked at him. He glanced around nervously, then bent toward his friends again. "So? I'm reading this book right now. It's called *The Spy Who Went Out for a Pizza*, and it's all about these KGB guys. They're nuts!"

"Weasel! Don't be a dope," Scott said. "There is no KGB anymore. There is no Soviet Union anymore! So why would they need spies?"

"I don't know!" Weasel hissed. "Maybe that's what they're trying to find out!"

"You're totally ridiculous," Megan said, rolling her eyes.

"She could be a spy herself!" Weasel insisted.

"Right," Vicki said. "And her assignment is to figure out what kind of meat they put in the cafeteria hamburgers."

Scott was distracted, looking at Manya. She was sitting alone at a table, eating soup and reading a book. Every once in a while, she looked around, but if

6

anyone caught her eye, she buried her nose in her book again. Her eyes were dark, and she had long, curly hair that sprang out from under her red beret. She looked . . .

"Beautiful," Scott said out loud.

"Scott! My man! You don't know what you're saying!" Weasel grabbed his arm. "She could be a spy! You don't know what she's capable of!"

"Weas, she's a pretty girl!" Scott said, exasperated.

"Right," Weasel grumbled. "So was Mata Hari."

"Mata who-y?" Vicki asked.

"Mata Hari," Weasel said, slowly and solemnly. "The most infamous female spy that ever lived."

"Hey, you guys, what's up?" Lindsay and Tommy D. appeared suddenly next to the table.

"Scott and Weasel were just arguing about that girl over there," Vicki said. "Scott thinks she's pretty, but Weasel thinks she's a Russian spy."

"Weasel, you have *got* to get out of the house more often," Tommy said, punching his arm playfully.

"Ow!" Weasel rubbed his arm.

"Ugh, look at you two," Vicki moaned. "You guys are the only people who are lucky in love in this whole school! You'll probably be the one happy couple at the big dance next week."

Tommy raised an eyebrow and eyed Scott as Vicki finished her sentence. Everyone knew that Scott had tried to steal Lindsay away from Tommy when he first started at Bayside, and Tommy was always ready for some kind of comment.

But Scott just crossed his arms and smiled at Tommy and Lindsay. "Yeah, you guys are kind of cute together," he said, nodding.

Tommy was impressed. Maybe Scott was finally getting the message that Lindsay was *his* girl.

"Oh, forget about the dance. I've got the greatest news!" Lindsay interrupted.

"They're going to start serving milk shakes in the cafeteria?" Weasel asked.

"Weasel, I'm serious!"

"So was I! You said it was the greatest news," Weasel pouted.

"Just ignore him," Megan said, grabbing Lindsay's arm. "Tell us. What's up?"

"Well"—Lindsay put her book down on the table and put her hands on her hips—"Mr. Belding called me into his office today."

"Yikes!" Weasel yelped. "And you came out alive?" Even though he was a model student, Weasel had a deep-seated fear of Mr. Belding. None of his friends really understood this fear.

8

"And he told me to sit down. . . , " Lindsay continued.

"In the chair of death?" Weasel squeaked.

"And he said he had to tell me something really important."

"I can't listen! It's too terrifying!" Weasel put his fingers in his ears and began humming the "Jeopardy" theme song. "Doo dee doo doo doo dee doo, doo dee doo dee *doop* do do-do-do-do—"

"Weasel!" Scott yelled, pulling his friend's fingers out of his ears. "Would you let Lindsay tell her story?"

"Sorry," Weasel said, sitting on his hands.

"Well to sum it all up: You are looking at the new editor in chief of the *Bayside Beacon*!" Lindsay said, grinning.

"Whoa! That is awesome!" Vicki said.

"You're the editor in chief of the school paper? That's really great!" Megan agreed.

"Yep—I'm the boss!" Lindsay said. "And I need everyone's help if we're going to whip the paper back into shape."

"That's a big job, Lindsay," Megan said. "We all know the paper's been pretty weak since Nosy Parker graduated last year."

"There was someone named Nosy who went to school here?" Scott asked in disbelief.

9

"That wasn't her *real* name," Vicki giggled. "Her name was Nanny. But she ran the whole paper, *and* she was the gossip columnist. She knew all the dirt on everyone."

"You guys, listen," Lindsay said, pulling out her notebook and sliding into an empty chair. "I need each of you to take on a job. I'm going to be the features editor. You know, I'll do all the human-interest stories. Scott and Vicki, I need you to be a team."

"Excellent!" Vicki said.

"Uh, Lindsay—," Scott began to protest.

"You two will be covering school news: new students, club activities, that kind of thing. Vicki, I especially need you to keep an eye out for health-and-environment news. Somehow I think you'll be good at that."

"That's great!" Vicki smiled and put her hand over Scott's. "Scott, I have a great idea for a story on sodium nitrates in the school-lunch hot dogs. Won't that be great? We could have lunch together every day!"

"Tommy, I need you to cover sports for me. And not just football, either!" Lindsay said, waving her pencil at him. "There's girls' lacrosse, ultimate Frisbee, wrestling—"

"Hey, I'm no writer!" Tommy protested.

"But you know sports, inside and out," Lindsay said soothingly. "Don't worry. I'll help you with the writing part. You'll learn really quickly."

She turned to Weasel. "Weas, you're in charge of desktop production. Figure out how to use the computers to make the paper look really jazzy."

"Whatever you say, chief." Weasel saluted.

"And Megan, I want you to do the horoscopes," Lindsay finished, making a check mark in her notebook.

"Hang on, Lindsay," Megan said. "I'm planning on being valedictorian. I can't be writing about stars and planets and all that flaky stuff!"

"But Megan, you have such a great imagination. Please?" Lindsay begged.

Megan and Lindsay began arguing back and forth about the astrology column.

Meanwhile, Vicki was scooting closer to Scott. "You know, Scott," she said, "we should really go to the library together, too, so we can look up all the technical names of food additives."

"*Lindsay!*" Scott yelled, louder than he meant to. Everyone stared at him.

"Uh, I was just thinking," he said quickly. "I'd love to do the horoscope, if Megan wants to switch with me."

"Scott! You're cool!" Megan's face lit up with a smile. "That's really nice of you."

Vicki sighed and rested her chin on her hand. Scott had escaped again! *Oh well*, she thought. *It was worth a shot.*

"Okay, Scott," Lindsay agreed. "You do the horoscopes. I don't know why you want to do it, but Megan sure doesn't want to, so it's all yours."

Everyone at the table began chatting excitedly about their new jobs on the school newspaper, forgetting about the Halloween dance.

Scott leaned back, put his hands behind his head, and thought for a minute. He was glad he'd gotten out of teaming up with Vicki. She was a nice girl and all, but she was obsessed with health and allergies. It could get a little annoying.

Still, he didn't yet know what he was going to do with this horoscope assignment. . . . Or did he? Scott's mind began to whir.

He kind of owed his new friends some good deeds. His planning and scheming had gotten them pretty mad at him last month. He accidentally gave Tommy an eye disease, then, when it looked as if he had a chance to date Lindsay, ditched Vicki and really hurt her feelings. It would be great to earn their trust by doing something nice for them. Something selfless—something noble.

Couldn't he use the horoscope column to help his friends? Maybe to match them up with the perfect dates for the Halloween dance? *Everybody reads their horoscope*, he thought. *It's almost like an advice column.* And a little advice in the right places could convince his friends that their dates were written in the stars!

chapter

A week later, Scott strolled into the office of the *Bayside Beacon*. It wasn't much of an office—just an empty classroom, with old posters of Christopher Columbus still up on the back wall. But in the past week it had become a hub of activity. Big tables replaced the desks, the walls were covered with schedules and story ideas, and piles of paper were everywhere.

Right now the office was empty, except for Vicki and a guy that Scott had never seen before. The two of them were bent over a table, arranging and rearranging a stack of note cards.

"Hey, Needleman!" Scott said.

"Oh, hi, Scott," Vicki answered, barely looking up. Scott was surprised. *What's going on here?* he thought. *Usually I have to peel Vicki off me.*

"What are you guys working on?" he asked.

Vicki looked up at him again, then gathered the note cards into a stack and tapped them on the table a few times. "Can you keep a secret?" she asked.

"Uh . . . sure," Scott said, getting curious.

"Okay," Vicki answered. "Scott, this is Bruce McKeone."

"Hi," Bruce said.

"Bruce is helping me uncover the biggest scam in the history of Bayside," Vicki said secretively.

"Uh-huh?" Scott asked.

"Yes. We have all kinds of evidence that's going to blow the lid off this school. We have conclusive proof of some very dirty dealings in the school cafeteria!"

"Isn't she incredible?" Bruce sighed and looked at Vicki adoringly.

"Thanks, Bruce." Vicki smiled at him. Then she sneezed. "Oops. I think that cream you put on your hives is bothering my mucous membranes," she said apologetically.

Hives? Mucous membranes? Scott made a face.

"Oh, I'm sorry, Vicki," Bruce said. "I'll use something different. It's just that this office is full of airborne irritants."

"I know," Vicki said sympathetically. She patted his arm.

Scott had to hide a grin as the truth suddenly hit him. Bruce obviously had a major crush on Vicki—and it looked like maybe she was interested in him, too! But it would be a good idea to hang around and make sure. If Scott's suspicions were confirmed, he might not have to fend her off anymore—and he could cross her off his list of friends who needed dates for the big dance.

"So, uh, Vicki, what kind of dirty dealings are you talking about?" Scott asked.

"Just check out these photographs!" Vicki said excitedly. She pulled out a plastic sheath of slides and held them up to the light so that Scott could get a good look.

"Here you can clearly see one problem." Vicki pointed at one picture.

"What? It's a cafeteria lady and she's wearing gloves," Scott protested.

"Look closer. Those gloves are petroleum-based," Vicki said. "Germs *cling* to those gloves. Not only that—her hair isn't even in a net."

"But Vicki, that's not her hair. It's a *wig*!" Scott said. "Everyone knows she wears a wig!"

"That makes it even worse!" Vicki replied emphatically. "Wigs are made of synthetic fibers. One of those synthetic hairs in your hamburger, and your intestines would never let you forget it. And look at this one," she went on, pointing to another slide.

"She's not doing anything wrong. She's just opening a can of tuna," Scott said.

"But she didn't rinse the top of the can first," Vicki pointed out. "Look at all that dust and dirt."

"There are many microorganisms that gather on the tops of cans," Bruce added. "At the very least, a can should be run under hot water before being opened, so the food inside doesn't become contaminated," he sniffed.

"Bruce really knows his contaminants," Vicki pointed out proudly.

"Yeah . . . great," Scott said, shaking his head. *Where did she find this guy?* he wondered. *He's as picky as she is.*

"Hey, we've got to motor if we're going to meet up with our informant," Bruce said, looking at his watch.

"Oh! Right," Vicki agreed. "We're meeting a secret informant in the parking lot under the school," she explained to Scott. "He's got exclusive information about the ingredients of mystery meat surprise."

"That sounds like a great story, Needleman," Scott said, but Vicki and Bruce were gone before he could even finish his sentence.

He sat down at the table and looked out the window. *This is great*, he thought. *It looks like Vicki is really hooking up with this guy!*

Then he had a frightening thought. Bruce was obsessed with his health. He had a million allergies. In fact, he was just like Vicki!

Vicki can be pretty ridiculous sometimes, but the rest of the gang keeps her clued in to reality, Scott thought. *But if she's paired up with this Bruce guy, he's just going to encourage her. Pretty soon, she'll be afraid to leave her house!*

This budding romance had to be stopped!

Just then the door opened, and Lindsay came into the office, reading something in a spiral notebook. Tommy D. was right behind her, and he looked anxious.

Lindsay sat down at a table by the door and looked at her boyfriend. Tommy D. paced nervously. Neither of them seemed to notice Scott. He sat in his chair in the corner, wondering whether he should say anything. But before he could make up his mind, Lindsay started talking.

18

"Tommy, maybe you should sit down," she said. Tommy sat. Lindsay drew in a deep breath. "Okay. The article is basically good. I mean, all the information is here, but there are some problems."

"Problems? What's wrong with it?" Tommy asked defensively.

"Nothing's wrong," Lindsay assured him. "But there's some stuff I want to change. For instance, I want to rearrange the information. It's kind of jumbled up, so it doesn't make much sense. And I'm going to jazz up the language a little, because it's kind of boring. And after that, I'm going to—"

"Wait a minute! I worked really hard on that article!" Tommy protested.

Scott felt bad for Tommy. He hadn't known the guy could look so hurt!

"That's great, Tommy, but I still have to make a few changes," Lindsay said.

"Like what?"

"Like I just told you. It's disorganized. You start off talking about the different members of the team. Then you switch to the team strategy. And you don't even mention who Bayside was playing against until halfway through the article!"

"Yeah, so?" Tommy said. His voice was starting to rise.

"Okay, let me explain it to you this way," Lindsay continued. "In this part of your article, you're talking about Sam Finnegan, the star player, making a really exciting play, and you say 'Sam jumped up. He made the shot. It was cool.' It's not a good idea to write like that in a newspaper article!"

"Why not?" Tommy was getting really mad.

"It's just not professional," Lindsay said, reaching over and squeezing her boyfriend's arm. "Tommy, please don't feel bad."

"Lindsay, I didn't even want this stupid sportswriting job, and now you're tearing apart everything I write!"

"Tommy—," Lindsay started, but Tommy was already out the door.

Scott jumped out of his seat and hurried after Tommy, ignoring Lindsay's startled look. "Tommy. Hey, Tommy D.!" he called.

Tommy D. stopped and turned around. "What do *you* want?" he growled. He obviously still didn't trust Scott.

"I heard what went on in there," Scott said. He felt a little awkward talking to Tommy like this, but he thought the guy could use some support, so he went on. "I know Lindsay sounded harsh, but she really didn't mean to be so critical. I don't think she realized you would feel so insecure about it."

"I'm not insecure," Tommy insisted. "But I told her—I'm no writer. I feel stupid having her read my writing. Now she thinks I'm a dope."

"If she thought you were a dope, she wouldn't be dating you," Scott said. "She must think you can do it, or she wouldn't have asked you to write for the paper. She's just being a good editor."

Tommy looked thoughtful. Then the office door opened, and Lindsay stuck her head out into the hall.

"Tommy?" She came over to him, her dark eyes round with worry. "I really don't want you to feel like I'm interfering with what you wrote. If it'll make you feel better, we'll leave the article just as it is."

Tommy hesitated for a minute. "Well, okay," he finally said, but he still looked doubtful.

Lindsay put her arms around his waist and leaned her head on his chest. "I didn't mean to hurt your feelings," she said.

"I know, Lindsay." Tommy put his arm around Lindsay, and they walked down the hall.

Scott grinned as he watched them go. *Okay*, he thought. *So they make a nice couple. Maybe Lindsay has a sister.*

Scott turned around to go back into the office, but he was stopped by the sound of a shrill whistle. He turned around, and his eyes widened as he saw Weasel leading a troop of five computer geeks around the corner.

While Weasel tooted on his whistle, the troop marched in formation through the door of the newspaper office and turned to the left, where there was a row of computers against the wall. Each person marched to a chair in front of a computer. At a long whistle blast from Weasel, they sat. And when Weasel tooted twice more, they sprang into action, unpacking sheafs of paper and piles of computer disks. A moment later they were typing furiously.

Scott was amazed. Five minutes before, the office had been practically empty, and now it looked like the war room at the Pentagon!

"Weasel, this is incredible!" Scott said, clapping the computer general on the back.

"Thanks, Scott," Weasel responded proudly. "This is it. My own kingdom. My world of computers, linking all of Bayside High in an electronic network of love."

"What are you talking about, man?" Scott asked. "I thought you were in charge of desktop publishing."

"That's a snap! This is an additional project I've

taken on," Weasel said. "Something Bayside's been begging for. The personals."

"You mean, where people send messages to other people without saying who they are?" Scott asked.

"Totally anonymous," Weasel confirmed. "Here, I'll show you." Weasel led Scott over to the first computer, which was beeping and buzzing as Jennifer, a skinny girl in a "Star Trek" T-shirt, tapped away at the keyboard.

"Behold!" Weasel said. "Jennifer here is retrieving personal messages from the computer network. We don't even know who sends these messages—they come in through the telephone lines. Totally private, totally secure."

"Here comes one now, Mr. Weasel," Jennifer said, hitting a button on the computer.

"*Mr.* Weasel?" Scott raised an eyebrow.

"These people look up to me," Weasel explained. "I'm in charge of this operation!" He bent closer to the screen and read the message.

"'To the cute guy with the blond ponytail who hangs out in the cafeteria,'" he read. "'I've been watching you. . . . Keep reading for more hints of who I am!' You see what I mean? People love this stuff. They need the personals!" Weasel walked triumphantly over to the next computer.

"Here comes another one. 'To the person who eats all the brownies out of the vending machine. Leave some for the rest of us!' Now, that's mysterious!"

Weasel moved down to the next computer and read the message to himself. Then he got pale and grabbed Scott by the arm.

"What does it say, Weasel?" Scott asked, trying to tug his arm free. "Too hot for the *Beacon*?"

"Too hot?" Weasel squeaked, tightening his grip. "It's a threat to democracy!"

"What are you talking about?" Scott asked, bending over to read the screen. "'CCCP—I'd kill for you!'" He straightened up. "So?"

"So?" Weasel was frantic. "I was reading another one of my spy novels last night—*I Spy with My Little Eye*. Don't you know what CCCP stands for?"

"Cheese, chicken, and chili pizza?" Scott cracked.

"This is no joking matter, Ericson. CCCP means USSR in Russian letters. USSR—as in the old Soviet Union."

"Weasel, you've got to be kidding me!" Scott said, laughing.

"Laugh all you want, Scottie boy." Weasel was serious. "This message was obviously sent by someone who feels so strongly about the Soviet Union that they would actually *kill* to see it back in power. And I'll just bet I know who it is!"

"Who?" Scott had to know.

"It's Manya, that girl from Russia!"

"Weas! You're flipping out!" Scott was laughing so hard that he had to wipe tears from his eyes. "Manya? She's just a kid!"

Weasel 'shook his head and stared at the screen. "She may look like she's just a kid," he said. "But I'll bet she was hardened by her years behind the Iron Curtain."

Scott clapped Weasel on the shoulder and shook him.

"You've been working too hard, Weasel," he said. "Come on down to the Max. I'm buying you a Max super-double cheeseburger surprise, okay?"

"That may solve the short-term problem," Weasel said mournfully as they left the office in the capable hands of the geek patrol. "But this may be the last meal we eat as free Americans."

chapter

3

The gang, gathered around a table at the Max,
exploded into laughter. Scott sat at the head of the
table, explaining Weasel's suspicions to Lindsay,
Megan, and Tommy.

"So I finally convinced him to come down to the
Max," Scott said, continuing the story. "But the whole
way down here, he just kept talking about spies and
Russia and Manya and cyanide pills and I don't know
what else. And just when we got to the door, he said
he had to get started on some investigation, and he
ran off!"

"Where was he going?" Megan asked, tucking a lock
of dark hair behind an ear.

"I think he was going home," Scott replied. "He said he was going to try to trap the spy!"

"Hey, should we be worried?" Lindsay asked. "Maybe we should try to go find him. Weasel could hurt himself!"

"I don't think we have to worry about finding him," Tommy said, nodding toward the door. "He just walked in."

They all looked toward the entrance to the Max. Weasel had just entered, all right, but he looked different. For one thing, he had changed his clothes. Earlier, he had been wearing a yellow Hawaiian shirt with brown jeans, white tube socks, and ratty sneakers. Now he was wearing a trench coat, an old-fashioned brown fedora, and black sunglasses. He wasn't acting like Weasel Wyzell, either. Instead of looking around frantically for his friends, he just looked left, then right, then walked slowly over to the table where his friends were sitting. He didn't even turn his head when he passed a table full of cheerleaders in uniform. He just eased himself into the booth and crossed his arms.

"Uh, Weasel?" Megan passed her hand over Weasel's sunglasses. "You in there?"

"Sssssshhhh," Weasel hissed. "You can't call me Weasel for a while. I'm going incognito."

27

"You're going in what?" Tommy asked.

"Incognito," Weasel explained impatiently. "No one can know I'm me. I'm trying to trap a spy."

"Weasel, be reasonable," Lindsay said. "You really don't have to do that. There aren't any spies at Bayside High."

Weasel leaned forward and lifted his glasses slightly so that he was peeking out from under them.

"My name is no longer Weasel," he whispered. "You must now refer to me as Special Agent Weazemeister. And Lindsay, don't kid yourself. I've been doing a lot of reading." He pulled a book out of his pocket. It was called *Spy-Guy*. "Unfortunately, the truth is ugly. There are spies"—he turned his head and looked around, then looked back at Lindsay—"everywhere. I've taken it upon myself to seek them out to make the world safe."

"Weasel, I think the Max is pretty safe," Tommy added.

Weasel dropped his glasses back down onto his nose. "Oh sure, you do," he intoned. "That's why I'm the spy, and you're the regular Joe."

"Regular Tommy, you mean," Lindsay giggled.

"Regular whatever," Weasel answered distractedly. "You guys can eat your little snacks and have your fun.

I'll be out somewhere, fighting the good fight. But don't worry about me. I don't mind. It's my mission."

Weasel stood slowly, put one finger to his lips, and then pointed to the opposite wall of the Max. Everyone turned around and looked, but there was nothing there. When they turned around again, Weasel had vanished.

"Oh, boy," Megan said. "Do you think he really believes all this spy stuff?"

"I don't know," Lindsay answered. "But I hope he's keeping up with his work on the *Beacon*. I mean, the first issue comes out tomorrow. Which reminds me— we should all get to the office to finish up!"

"You guys go ahead," Scott announced, picking up his books. "I'll meet you there later. I just have some business to take care of."

"All right, Scott, but we're counting on you," Lindsay said.

"I won't let you down. My horoscope column is really going to be something special," Scott promised.

While the rest of the gang were getting their books together, Scott headed for Mr. Belding's office.

One of the secretaries, Ms. Sansone, was sitting at her desk. Most of the school was afraid of Ms. Sansone. She was about Mr. Belding's age—middle-aged—and she had sort of a permanent frown under caked-on makeup. But Scott was not the kind of guy to let a frown get in his way. One of his first projects when he came to Bayside had been to stop by and talk to Ms. Sansone. It turned out that she was kind of a nice lady, once you got her talking about her cats.

"Oh, hi, Scott," she said brightly.

"Hey, Ms. Sansone," Scott replied, turning on his famous Ericson charm. "How's old Tinkerbell holding up?"

"Oh, Tink is doing fabulously," she said, smiling. She handed him a picture of a fluffy gray cat. "He didn't need an operation after all. The veterinarian just put him on a special diet."

"That's great," Scott said, handing the picture back to her. "I was pretty worried about Tink for a while there. Say, did you have a chance to . . . ?"

"Yes, I circulated those questionnaires you gave me." The secretary reached into her desk and pulled out a pile of papers. "I put them in each homeroom teacher's mailbox, and I told the teachers that Mr. Belding needed the information for the school records. Here you go."

"Thanks, Ms. Sansone. You're the greatest!"

"Oh, well—" She began to blush. "Never mind, Scott. It's my pleasure."

30

"See you later, Ms. Sansone," Scott said, waving cheerfully as he left the office.

Scott found an empty classroom and spread out the questionnaires to look them over. Each one had a space for the student's name and birth date. He separated them into astrological signs. Below the birth date, each sheet had information about what clubs the person belonged to, what sports she or he played, and what activities she or he thought the school should have.

Scott rubbed his hands happily. This was exactly the kind of information he needed to match people up! He could find people that had a lot in common, and then advise them—through the horoscope column—to get together.

Let's see, he thought. *The first thing I've got to do is get Vicki away from this Bruce guy.* Luckily, getting rid of Bruce would be easy. He found Bruce's questionnaire and looked it over.

Capricorn, he thought. *Okay, here goes.* Smiling to himself, he started writing:

Capricorn: Bad luck follows you like a cloud of pollen! Your health is in terrible danger. Stay indoors, preferably in bed, until the danger is past.

Since Bruce was as much of a hypochondriac as
Vicki, that would probably keep him in bed for *days*.
Now, who could Scott find to be Vicki's dream date?
He looked through the questionnaires in search of the
perfect candidate.

"Dave Williams," Scott said out loud, then read the
questionnaire over again. Biology Club and Future
Doctors of America. He was just the guy for Vicki.
She'd love to have a doctor around all the time! He
double-checked the dates of Dave's and Vicki's birth-
days. Dave was a Taurus and Vicki was a Libra. He
started writing again.

> Taurus: Today you'll do a good deed that will
> confirm you've chosen the right profession. Look
> for an attractive Libra who shares your interests.

Scott nodded, pleased with his plan. He looked at
his watch. He'd better finish up and go meet the rest of
his friends to put the paper together!

He had already taken care of his matchmaking job
for that week. Now he just needed to write some snap-
py advice for the other zodiac signs. He gave Aries
some general advice about being nice to strangers, and
he told Scorpio to do some extra credit for homework.

He had to work quickly, but it only took him about half an hour. This was easier than he had thought it would be! With his column complete, he hid the questionnaires in a folder and rushed out the door.

As he walked down the hall, Scott smiled to himself. It looked like his plan to get Vicki and Dave together had potential. Of course, there was a minor problem. Dave was pretty dedicated to scientific stuff, and he probably didn't put much stock in astrological predictions. Scott was going to have to figure out some way to make a true believer out of him. *But I'll worry about that later*, he thought as he rounded the corner near the newspaper office. *Right now I have a deadline.*

When Scott burst through the door of the office, everyone else was already there, running around busily.

"Scott! Great!" Lindsay grabbed his arm. "Do you have your horoscope column?"

"Right here," Scott said, handing it over.

"Super." She glanced at it, then did a double take. "'The Stars and You, by Madame Moussaka'?" she read aloud. "Scott, who in the world is Madame Moussaka?"

"It's an alias," Scott explained. "I don't want anyone

to know it's really *me* writing these predictions. If they knew the truth, they wouldn't take them seriously."

Lindsay shrugged. "Well, I guess it's all right. Whatever floats your boat." She handed the page to Weasel. "Okay, Weasel, do your stuff."

Weasel had taken off his spy gear long enough to help organize the paper. He cracked his knuckles, then quickly typed in the horoscopes.

"Here's my exposé on the cafeteria," Vicki announced, handing Weasel a disk as Bruce looked on admiringly.

"Uh, here's my sports article." Tommy gave Weasel a crumpled, dog-eared, erased-and-rewritten-on piece of paper.

"Hey!" Weasel piped up. "This is all messed up. I can barely read it!"

Tommy growled.

"Then again," Weasel squeaked, "it's messed up in a very *attractive* way. I like it!" He hunched over the computer and typed the article in.

Everyone gathered around the computer as Weasel rearranged the articles, fitting them on the various pages. Finally he was finished. He hit a key, and the first issue of the new *Bayside Beacon* printed out.

Everybody cheered. Lindsay grabbed the newspaper and held it over her head. Tommy D. picked her up and put her on the desk in the front of the room.

34

"You guys," she shouted, "it was rough, but we did it. Tomorrow, Bayside's going to be blown away by our awesome paper!"

Everybody high-fived and cheered again. Tommy D. and Lindsay hugged. The gang was so busy celebrating, nobody noticed as Weasel put his hat and shades back on and sneaked out the door.

chapter

—

"A Lava lamp! Who would throw this out? If you just scrape the banana peel off, it's as good as new!"

It was the next morning, and Scott and Weasel were hiding out behind the garbage cans in back of the school, waiting to put Scott's plan into action.

"Hey, I really appreciate you taking time out from your spy activities to help me," Scott said. sincerely.

"Scott, buddy, I may be the last hope for the American way of life, but I still remember my friends," Weasel replied. "Hey, look! Jujubes! And they haven't even been opened!"

"Weas, this is it. Here comes Dave Williams. Now, are you sure you told Homer what to do?"

"You betcha," Weasel assured Scott. "I told him to pretend to choke on a piece of gum right in front of Dave. Dave will do the Heimlich maneuver on him, and if it's all timed right, Vicki will be here to witness his heroic act!"

"Cool." Scott was satisfied. He pulled a copy of the *Bayside Beacon* out of his pocket. "'Today you'll do a good deed that will confirm you've chosen the right profession,'" he read from his horoscope column. "Saving Homer from choking should confirm that Dave'd make a great doctor! That should get him to believe his horoscope."

Weasel began fiddling with his watch, turning the little dials and pressing the little buttons that stuck out from its sides.

"Nice watch," Scott said, arching his eyebrows. It was awfully big and complicated-looking for a wrist-watch.

"Thanks," Weasel said, looking up briefly. "I ordered it from one of my spy catalogs." He poked at it a few more times, then smiled in satisfaction. "Okay," he said. "I've been doing extensive research on the habits of our friends to prepare for this moment. That's how I knew this was the place for Homer to pretend to choke. According to my research, at the sound of the tone, Vicki is scheduled to come around the northwestern corner of the school, while Dave should approach from the opposite vector."

Weasel's watch let out a high-pitched beep. Sure enough, as Scott watched, Vicki, Megan, and Lindsay came around the corner. Homer, a little guy with red hair parted in the middle, was sitting on a bench near the garbage cans. And from the other direction, Dave came walking, his books under his left arm.

Weasel and Scott watched breathlessly as Dave got closer to Homer. When he was about fifteen feet away, Homer started coughing. But Dave didn't notice.

After a few seconds, Homer started gagging louder. Dave stopped, but he just bent down to tie his shoes. Homer stood up and staggered around, clutching his throat. He staggered over to where Dave was standing, one arm outstretched. Dave still didn't see him. He finished tying his shoes and stood up.

Homer continued to stagger around, and he shot a panicked look at Weasel. Weasel motioned to him, and Homer fell to his knees right in front of Dave. Finally, Dave noticed him.

"Whoa! What's the matter, guy?" Dave asked. Homer was lying on his back, his eyes bulging out. He pulled a pack of gum out of his pocket and held it up, still gagging.

"Oh, no! Are you choking, man? Hey, you're choking!" Dave wasted no time. He bent down, picked Homer up, turned him around, hugged him around the waist, and brought his hands up sharply into Homer's abdomen. The gum shot out of Homer's mouth.

"Ow! That looked real!" Scott whispered.

"Don't worry," Weasel whispered back. "I told him to stick a notebook under his sweater so he wouldn't get hurt!"

They looked up again as Dave clapped Homer on the back. Homer had his hand on his chest and was breathing hard.

"You saved my life! Thank you! You're my hero!" Homer said, as loudly as he could, looking over at the girls. They came rushing over and started talking anxiously.

"Homer, are you okay?" Lindsay was asking.

Vicki turned to Dave. "That was awesome," she told him.

"It really was," Megan agreed.

Dave looked a little pale. "Oh, whatever," he said. "I just . . . It was something I learned in my Red Cross training class."

"Oh, are you a lifeguard?" Vicki asked, sounding impressed.

"No, I want to be a doctor," Dave said. "So I thought lifesaving classes would be good preparation."

"Wow," the girls all said together.

"I've got to get to Biology class," Dave said. He turned to Homer again. "Are you sure you're okay?"

Homer rubbed his belly. "Oh, I'm as good as new. Thanks, Dave."

"Okay," Dave said. "I'll catch you later." He picked up his books and walked toward the school. The girls all watched him go, and Homer walked off in the other direction, pulling his notebook out from under his shirt as he went.

Weasel and Scott saw the girls watching Dave and gave each other a high five.

"Weasel, you're awesome!" Scott said. "That worked perfectly. Dave has got to believe his horoscope now!"

"Scott, I'm glad I could be of help to you," Weasel said. Becoming a spy again, he clapped his hat back onto his head and put on his shades. "But duty calls. I have some major investigations to complete." Suddenly he gasped and pointed. "Oh, look! It's Cindy Crawford!"

Scott whipped his head around to see the supermodel. No one was there. When he turned around again, Weasel was gone. All that was left was a soggy, unopened box of jujubes.

"I wish he would stop disappearing like that," Scott muttered to himself as he picked up his books. He picked the trash off his sneakers and headed back into the school.

Meanwhile, the girls were still standing in a cluster, talking about Dave's heroic act.

"I didn't know that Dave was planning to be a doctor!" Vicki said, hugging her books to her chest.

"It looks like he's already started saving lives," Lindsay said. "That was really cool, the way he saved Homer like that."

The bell for first period rang, and Vicki jumped.

"Oh, no! I'm supposed to meet with my English teacher before class! I've gotta run. See you guys at lunch?"

"Okay, we'll see you then," Lindsay called after her. Vicki was already pulling open the school door.

"You're awfully quiet, Megan," Lindsay said as the two girls walked to class together. "What's up?"

"I'm just thinking about what Dave did," Megan said seriously. "It really took a lot of guts. I wouldn't have known what to do."

"Yeah, it really was amazing," Lindsay agreed.

"I mean, it's one thing to take a lot of science cours- es and talk about being a doctor," Megan continued. "But he really thinks about what it would be like to save lives, and he goes out and does it!"

"Well, I guess so," Lindsay said, looking curiously at Megan.

"I just . . . I can't believe he was so quick, and he knew what to do!"

"Megan!" Lindsay stopped short and grabbed her friend by the arm. "Do I smell a crush brewing?"

Megan blushed. "Okay. I admit it. I see Dave all the time in the library, and I always thought he was sort of cute. But I think my crush just got serious!"

"Oh, cool!" Lindsay said, linking her arm in Megan's. "You guys would make a perfect couple. You're both so smart."

"Now, keep this quiet, Lindsay!" Megan warned. "I don't want to be like Vicki and start mooning around and fluttering my eyelashes at some guy just because I like him. I want to play it cool, okay?"

"Okay, okay!" Lindsay assured her friend. "My lips

are sealed." She was quiet for a minute. Then she started giggling. "But I'm so excited for you!"

Megan tried to keep a straight face, but then she started giggling, too. She might just have a date for the dance after all!

By lunchtime, the whole school was in an uproar. The *Bayside Beacon* was a hit, all right—and now nobody would eat in the cafeteria!

Hundreds of kids were sitting in the hallway outside the kitchen. A few people had brought bag lunches, and they were busily cutting up their peanut-butter sandwiches and carrot sticks to share with the rest of the hungry students. On the other side of the doors, the cafeteria ladies were standing there with nothing to do. One of them stuck her head out into the hall.

"Aw, come on, kids, it's not that bad," she called out.

"Forget it!" someone yelled back. "We're not eating that food. We won't even eat in that room until you clean up your act!"

"But it's not us," the lady responded. "We're just following school orders!"

"Well, we think it's a disgrace!" another girl yelled, waving a copy of the *Beacon*. The headline, splashed across the front page in huge block letters, said CHEZ BAYSIDE: IF IT WERE A RESTAURANT, IT WOULD BE CONDEMNED!

Megan and Lindsay stood at the end of the hall, surrounded by people reading the *Beacon*. Lindsay seemed a little worried.

"Are you okay?" Megan asked, putting a hand on Lindsay's arm.

"Yeah, I guess so," Lindsay answered. "I just never thought the school newspaper would have this much of an effect on people. If anyone gets in trouble, it's really my fault."

"Why?" Megan asked.

"I'm in charge of the paper! If I hadn't let Vicki write that article, this wouldn't be happening." Lindsay bit her lower lip nervously.

"Well . . . it's not *that* bad," Megan said, trying to make her friend feel better. "I mean, it's just a few people who don't feel like eating in the cafeteria. It's not like the whole school is affected."

Just then, all the guys from the football team and the soccer team ran into the hallway, carrying a huge banner that read, BAYSIDE STUDENTS FOR BETTER FOOD! Everyone cheered as they hung the banner on the wall. They were followed by six students from the Latin Club, holding up a sign in Latin. Megan couldn't read Latin, but she guessed it was a translation of the athletes' slogan.

"Okay, so maybe a lot of people are involved," Megan admitted. "But I'm sure it'll blow over soon."

"Hey, Mr. Belding's coming!" one of the cheerleaders yelled. The hallway got even louder as people began talking nervously. It was one thing to refuse to eat in the cafeteria, but now the principal was on his way!

"Uh-oh," Lindsay muttered. She was really getting anxious.

Bayside's principal came barreling down the hall and stood in the doorway of the cafeteria. His round face was bright red—almost purple—and his thinning hair was sticking straight up. He was holding a copy of the *Beacon*. After looking at the students' faces, he held up his hands to quiet the mob.

"All right, all right," he shouted, as the hallway gradually quieted down. "What seems to be the problem here?"

"We don't want to eat in there! It's gross," a small voice piped up.

"That's Emily Simon," Megan whispered. "She's so shy, I don't think I've ever heard her speak before!"

"I know you're all concerned about this article," he announced, holding up the front page.

Everyone shouted their agreement.

"I just want to assure you that the problem is being looked into," he continued. "Meanwhile, won't you please go eat in the lunchroom?"

For the first time, the hallway was silent.

"Please?" Mr. Belding looked desperate. No one moved.

"All right, all right! I'll have this taken care of immediately. But I think you people are ridiculous!" he shouted, striding down the hallway toward his office.

Everyone cheered and tossed their newspapers into the air.

"Hey, cub reporters, what's the scoop?"

Megan and Lindsay turned around to see Vicki standing behind them. She was wearing a hat with a card that said PRESS sticking up out of it.

"Scoop?" Megan asked.

"You know," Vicki said. "The big story. The newest news. The scoop! What's up?"

"Vicki!" Lindsay took Vicki's hat off and clutched it to her chest, crushing it. "What's up is that the whole school is going crazy!"

"Hey! Give me that back," Vicki said, grabbing her hat and smoothing it out. "The truth is not always pretty. But when I get a hot lead, I've got to stop the presses and tell it like it is." She put her hat back on. "It's my duty as a journalist."

"You wrote one story," Megan pointed out. "That doesn't make you a journalist. Don't you think maybe you're getting a little carried away?"

"Megan, this newspaper is the best thing that ever happened to me!" Vicki said dramatically. "I feel like I have a new purpose. I would sacrifice everything for this!" She shook a copy of the *Beacon* in Megan's face. Then she sneezed. "Even if the ink *is* a proven toxin," she added. "Now if you'll excuse me, I have to look into the fumes given off by the varnish used on the gym floor."

Vicki waved good-bye as she strode down the hallway. Megan and Lindsay watched her go, dumbfounded.

48

"I think I've created a monster," Lindsay said gloomily.

o o o

Weasel was walking down the hallway at Bayside, near the public telephones, when he heard something strange. A female voice was talking on the phone—but was that English she was speaking? Or was it Russian?

He ducked around the corner and listened to the voice. Then he reached into his backpack and grabbed one of his new pieces of spy equipment—a periscope. If he looked into one end, he could see around the corner, thanks to the arrangement of mirrors in the gadget. He held the periscope up to his eye and slid it down the wall so that he could see who was talking on the phone.

It took a lot of adjustment, but he finally got a clear view. It was Manya, all right! She was talking excitedly on the phone, in English with a heavy Russian accent. He listened carefully, but she was talking in a low voice, and with that accent, it was hard to understand. He couldn't catch every word.

"He will be here next Friday?" she asked. She sounded agitated. "All the way from Moscow? Does he know I am here?"

She listened some more.

"I can't believe it," she responded to whatever the other person said on the phone. "I am going to kill him!"

Weasel was so shocked that he dropped the periscope. Was Manya getting her instructions from the KGB, right here at Bayside? It sounded like she was getting orders to murder an important visitor from Russia!

While he was stooping to pick up the periscope, Manya said something else to the person on the other end of the telephone. Unfortunately, Weasel couldn't hear it. Then she hung up and walked briskly away.

Weasel stuffed his spy gear back into his backpack and headed up the stairs, toward the library. He had to take a look at the town newspapers. Were any important Russian visitors coming to Palisades?

If there were, he had to protect them from Manya!

o   o   o

Scott leaned contentedly against his locker, watching everyone read the *Beacon*. His method of using people's personal interests to write the horoscopes seemed to be working. He had already overheard three people talking about how eerily on-target the predictions were. Everyone was taking it pretty seriously!

The final test still remained, though. Scott needed to know if his plan to match up Dave Williams and Vicki Needleman was going to work. He was waiting for Dave to walk by so that he could see how it was going. Finally, Dave came around the corner.

"Hey, Dave!" Scott called out, waving. Dave waved back and walked over.

"I heard what you did for Homer this morning," Scott said, clapping him on the back. "Great work!"

"Oh, thanks," Dave said, grinning. "It's all in a day's work for a future doctor. But you know what's really weird?"

"What?" Scott asked.

"Well, I read my horoscope in the school newspaper this morning in homeroom, and it said that something like this would happen!"

"No kidding!" Scott said, letting out a whistle. *This is great*, he thought. *My plan is really going to work!* "The horoscopes, huh? Gee, I never put much stock in them up till now, but I guess they really do have some truth to them!"

"Yeah, right," Dave said, laughing and shaking his head. "You're funny, Scott." He looked back and forth down the hall, then leaned toward Scott.

"There was something I wanted to talk to you

about, though," he said. "You know that big Halloween dance that's coming up?"

"Oh, yeah, I heard a buzz about it," Scott said, getting more and more excited. "Why do you ask?"

"Well, I was thinking of asking someone. I've seen you talking to her, and I thought you could help me out," Dave said confidentially.

Scott leaned towards Dave, nodding. "I knew it," he said.

"You did?" Dave asked, looking puzzled.

"Yes. Absolutely," he said. He patted Dave on the shoulder. "I think you two would make a great pair."

"Great!" Dave said, shrugging. He seemed pleased. "So you'll talk to Megan for me?"

"Megan!" Scott practically dropped his books.

Dave frowned in confusion. "Yeah, Megan," he said. "Who else would I be talking about?"

"Oh, I don't know," Scott said, trying to figure out where his plan could have gone wrong. "But isn't she a Gemini?"

"A *what*?" Dave asked, squinting his eyes at Scott.

"A Gemini," Scott said, pulling a copy of the paper out of his back pocket. "Look. The horoscope that said you would do a good deed today also says you should look for a Libra."

"Uh, Scott, buddy," Dave said, carefully refolding the paper and putting it back into Scott's hands. "You don't really believe this stuff, do you?"

"Well, I don't know," Scott said. "I mean, it was right about the first part. You can't be too careful."

"Scott, this is all made-up! It was just a coincidence that it said that in my horoscope. Man, you've got to get serious!" Dave laughed and walked away. Scott stared after him, stricken.

"Scott? Are you okay?" Scott turned around and saw Lindsay.

"I don't know," Scott admitted, putting his hands into his jeans pockets. "I think I may have gotten myself in trouble again."

Lindsay sighed, her brown eyes full of concern. She really liked Scott—as a friend—and she was glad that he had transferred to Bayside. But he was always up to some kind of scam. Sometimes she worried about the trouble he got himself into.

"What is it this time?" she asked as they started walking down the hall. "Did you get caught moving Mr. Belding's parking-space sign over to the dumpster again?"

They both laughed. Mr. Belding had a special parking space, right by the entrance to the school, marked with a green-and-white sign that said MR. BELDING PARKS HERE. Scott had moved that sign earlier in the year, and had gotten into trouble because of the prank.

"No, it's not like that," Scott explained. "I'm trying to do something *good* this time, but it's not working out."

"Well, what is it?" Lindsay asked. "Maybe I can help."

Scott thought for a minute. He didn't want Lindsay to know exactly what he was up to. Her friends were involved, and she might not approve of the way he was trying to rig things—even though he was sure she'd approve of the results! But it couldn't hurt to tell her what the general situation was. Maybe she *could* help.

"I wanted to help a friend of mine get a date for the dance. You know, the *right* date," he explained. "So I've been using my job on the newspaper to sort of push things along. I got her to like him. And then I wrote a horoscope for this guy, hinting at him to ask this girl out. The trouble is, he just doesn't believe in horoscopes."

Lindsay looked exasperated. "Scott, haven't you learned *anything*?" she asked, smacking him with her notebook. "These schemes of yours never work! And besides, matchmaking always backfires. You have to let things happen naturally."

54

"But I know exactly how to fix it in my next horoscope column," Scott assured her.

"Look, Scott. I don't know what you're up to, and I'm not sure I want to . . . unless you're going to tell me?"

Scott shook his head. "I can't tell you anything else," he said.

"Fine. Then here's my advice. Don't be a goofball!" Lindsay answered. "Just let it be. You don't need to fix anyone up!"

Scott was about to answer, when Tommy D. came around the corner. He didn't look happy.

"Tommy—oh my gosh, I was supposed to meet you!" Lindsay gasped. "I forgot, and now I have to get to a meeting with Mr. Belding! I'm so sorry!" She slipped an arm around his waist and looked up at him.

"Don't worry about it," Tommy said, pulling back a bit and avoiding her eyes. "I need to talk to Scott anyway."

"Oh!" Lindsay looked surprised and a little hurt. It was unusual for Tommy not to hug her back. "Okay. Um, I'll see you after school, all right?"

"Sure." Tommy kissed the top of her head and gave her a little squeeze. Lindsay looked at him for a second. Then she went slowly up the stairs toward the newspaper office.

Scott looked carefully at Tommy D. He was holding a copy of the *Beacon*, which looked as if it had been folded and unfolded about a hundred times.

"What's up, Tommy?" Scott asked.

"It's this stupid paper," Tommy said, handing it to Scott.

"Looks okay to me," Scott said. "I hear the horoscopes are pretty accurate."

"I don't care about the horoscopes. Look at my article," Tommy D. said, turning the paper over. "Everyone's making fun of me. I can't write."

Scott scanned the sports section, reading Tommy's writing. He hated to admit it, but the writing was pretty terrible. Tommy cared about what he was reporting on, but all his sentences came out wrong. Nothing really made sense; and on top of that, it was boring to read.

Scott thought back to Lindsay and Tommy's fight in the newspaper office. Lindsay had said she would leave the article alone to make Tommy feel better, and she had—but it made Tommy feel worse when everyone made fun of him. Scott gave him a sympathetic look. Tommy had a problem, all right.

56

"Well, maybe this article's not going to win you the Pulitzer Prize for journalism, but it's okay," Scott said. "So what do you need me for?"

Tommy D. shifted his weight and looked out the window. Then he switched his notebook to his right hand, and back to his left. Then he scratched his head.

"Come on, man, spit it out!" Scott said encouragingly. "Do you want me to talk to Lindsay? Do you want me to put a stink bomb in the locker of someone who made fun of you?"

Tommy D. shook his head. "I hate to ask you this," he said. "I mean, we're not exactly best friends. But you're the only one I can think of who could help me. You're a smart guy, and you do good in English and everything. But you can't tell anyone."

"My lips are sealed—but I can't help you unless you tell me what you're talking about!" Scott said.

Tommy shifted his weight again, and finally dropped the bomb. "I need you to give me writing lessons," he blurted out.

6

I suppose you're all wondering why I've called you here," Mr Belding said. He was pacing back and forth behind his desk. It was the Monday following the publication of the new *Bayside Beacon's* premiere issue.

The entire newspaper staff—Scott, Tommy D., Lindsay, Megan, Vicki, and Weasel—were sitting on the seats and arms of the leather chairs in Mr. Belding's office. Everyone was nervous. Vicki was still wearing her PRESS hat, but even she looked a little worried. Weasel looked as if he were about to faint.

"Mr. Belding," Lindsay interrupted, "I'm really sorry about the cafeteria thing. I'll try not to get you in trouble again."

58

Spilling the Beans

"Ms. Warner, please, I am quite over the cafeteria scandal," Mr. Belding said, smiling.

Everyone breathed a sigh of relief.

"I had forgotten what power the press has," he continued, sitting on the edge of his desk. "You probably won't believe this, but I was on the school newspaper when I was in high school. And it's been a long time since I've seen people pay as much attention to a problem within our school as they did after your cafeteria story, and it really got me thinking. Students should understand the power of the press—and the power of their fellow students!"

"That's great, Mr. Belding, but what does that have to do with us?" Lindsay asked, frowning in puzzlement.

"Well, Lindsay, up until now the *Beacon* has always come out every other week. But you are doing such a bang-up job, I've decided that it should come out every week!"

"Every week?" Lindsay sat up suddenly. "But Mr. Belding, that's twice as much work!"

"I knew you'd love the idea," Mr. Belding said, beaming. "That's why I already made the announcement to the superintendent that we would be doing this. The new edition is due this Friday!"

"Mr. Belding, I'm really glad that you like the paper

59

so much," Lindsay said, "but this is totally unexpected! I have a big English paper due this Friday. I don't know if I have time to put out another *Beacon* so soon!"

"I've already made arrangements with your teachers," Mr. Belding reassured her. "You have special permission to work on the paper during study halls, and you'll be given extensions on tests and papers if necessary."

"Well, I guess. . . . " Lindsay trailed off, looking uncertain.

Mr. Belding smiled. "I've seen what you've done with the paper already, and I *know* you're up to the challenge, Lindsay," he said. "I have faith in you!"

"And we'll help you, Lindsay," Megan said encouragingly.

"Yeah," Vicki agreed. "I've already got an amazing idea for us to work on."

"Okay then," Lindsay said. "We'll do it!"

"This is going to be awesome," Weasel said, rubbing his hands together. "I'll just hook a few more computers into my network!"

Everyone was excited and happy. Everyone, that is, except Tommy D. He looked miserable and nervous.

Scott was the last one out of Mr. Belding's office.

Suddenly someone grabbed him by the arm and pulled him into an empty classroom.

"Hey—let me go!" he yelled. "Whatever I did, I'm sorry!"

He felt someone let go of him, and he turned around. It was Tommy D., and Scott breathed a sigh of relief.

"Sorry," Tommy D. apologized. "I just didn't want anyone to see us leaving together. Can you help me with my writing now?"

"Sure," Scott said, looking around. "Here? Don't you want to go to the library or something?"

"No way," Tommy said firmly. "I don't want Lindsay to know I had to get help from someone."

"There's nothing wrong with needing a little help," Scott pointed out.

"Maybe not for you," Tommy responded.

"Okay. Let me see what you wrote," Scott offered.

Scott looked over the article that Tommy had written. It was about football.

"'The football team played an away game on Saturday. It was a tough game, but we won. The offense played really good,'" he read aloud. He looked up.

"Well?" Tommy D. demanded. "How do I make it better?"

"Well, if you want, I can rewrite it for you," Scott offered.

Tommy tossed a pen against the wall, exasperated. "That's not the point, Ericson. I'm supposed to be doing this myself. I just want you to tell me what to do!"

"Well . . ." Scott thought for a minute. "You're using a lot of words that are pretty basic. Maybe you should use a thesaurus."

"What is that—a dinosaur?" Tommy asked.

Scott laughed . . . until he realized Tommy wasn't kidding. "Uh, no, it's not a dinosaur," Scott explained. "It's like a dictionary, but instead of the definition, it tells you different words that you can use."

"Different words?"

"Yeah—so like, instead of *run*, you could say *race* or *hurry*," Scott said patiently. "The thesaurus would tell you that."

"Okay." Tommy looked thoughtful. "I'll look in a thesaurus. What else?"

"Well, maybe you could use metaphors, so you don't keep saying the same thing over and over," Scott suggested.

"Meta-whats?"

Scott sighed. "Metaphors," he said. "So like,

instead of saying, 'We played a football game against the Falcons,' you could say, 'We waged war on the Falcons.' That's a metaphor."

Tommy stared blankly at Scott, confused.

"Look," Scott continued. "When I write the horoscopes, I could just say, 'You're going to have a good day.' But then no one would want to read it, you know?"

"I guess," Tommy said, shrugging.

"But you can say the same thing and be creative about it. So I can say, 'You will have an amazingly great day.' Or maybe I can get even fancier, and say, 'Nowhere does your luck shine brighter than through the sun's sparkling rays.' That's a metaphor."

"You mean, because it's going to be sunny, it'll be a good day?" Tommy asked.

Scott sighed again. "No. I mean, it might be sunny, but it's a horoscope column, not the weather report. But the good luck is going to feel as good as sunshine feels. That's why you say it's the sun's sparkling rays."

"Oh," Tommy said thoughtfully. "I get it. Yeah. A metaphor." Tommy grinned.

"Okay. So you can use other words, and you can use metaphors. You can also describe other things besides just the players and the game."

"What else is there?" Tommy looked confused again.

"Well, you want people who weren't at the game to feel as if they were there," Scott explained. "So you can tell them what the playing field looked like, and how many people were in the bleachers. Stuff like that."

"And what the weather was like?" Tommy asked anxiously.

"Yeah, okay, you can say what the weather was like. Like, 'It was a dark and stormy day, and the Bayside team shivered on the sidelines while they waited for the challengers to arrive.'"

"Whoa," Tommy said, nodding gravely. "That sounds serious."

"Well, that's the kind of stuff you can do to spice up your sportswriting," Scott said, patting Tommy's shoulder encouragingly. "So do you want to go over the whole article together, and I'll make some suggestions?"

"No." Tommy stood up. "I think I've got a handle on it now. I'm going to rewrite this article myself." He nodded at Scott. "Thanks a lot, man."

Tommy walked out of the classroom, and Scott breathed a sigh of relief. He hoped he had been helpful. But turning Tommy D. into a star reporter was probably a bigger job than he could handle!

o   o   o

Weasel was excited about the paper, all right, but he had bigger fish to fry. He had been doing some investigative research into the idea of a Soviet spy at Bayside, and he was thoroughly convinced that it was Manya. Now he just had to investigate her. When school let out, he put on his spy clothes—trench coat, hat, and sunglasses—and waited for Manya to pass by.

When the last-period bell sounded, students poured out through the front doors. Weasel watched carefully, but he didn't see Manya. He began to think that he had missed her, and he checked his clunky black wristwatch several times before she finally came out, all by herself.

She sure is gorgeous—I mean, suspicious, Weasel thought as he began following her down the street.

Suddenly Manya made a sharp turn and headed into a store. *Ah-ha!* Weasel thought. *Maybe she knows I'm following her. I'll have to put on my other disguise.* He pulled a pair of thick glasses with a fake nose and mustache out of his trench-coat pocket and put it on. He smiled suavely at his reflection in the store window. *There. Now she won't know it's me.*

Manya came out of the store with a box of computer disks and continued down the street. Weasel kept shadowing her, staying even closer than before. She stopped suddenly outside another store, and he almost bumped into her.

"That was close," he muttered to himself as she went into the store. "She sure is buying a lot of stuff." He was pretty sure she hadn't noticed him, but just in case, he took off the glasses and put on another disguise: earmuffs.

It was kind of warm for earmuffs—in fact, since Palisades was in southern California, it was almost *always* kind of warm for earmuffs. Soon sweat was trickling down Weasel's neck. But he wasn't complaining. He was prepared to make even bigger sacrifices in the line of duty!

After a few minutes, Manya came out again, with a small plastic bag. Weasel continued to follow her. She made a few more sudden turns, and suddenly Weasel realized she was going into the Max.

Good thing I've got my disguise in place, he thought. *Now I have a perfect opportunity to question this suspect without her recognizing me from school.*

Manya sat by herself at a small table in the corner. The waitress came over, took her order, and left again. When it looked like the coast was clear, Weasel sidled up to her table and sat down.

"I hope you don't mind if I join you," he said, narrowing his eyes commandingly at her. "I find you . . . fascinating."

Manya gasped and blushed. She looked down. Then she looked back up. "N-no, I don't mind if you sit," she said in a lilting Russian accent.

She looks like she thinks something weird is happening, Weasel thought. *That's very suspicious. She must feel guilty about her spy activities.*

He adjusted his earmuffs and continued the conversation. "So," he said, drumming his fingers on the table. "I notice you have an accent. Are you from . . . France?"

"Ah, no," Manya said, giggling. "Not France. I am from Russia, where it used to be the Soviet Union. My family came to America this year. I like it very much."

Now it was Weasel's turn to be startled. He had been sure she would lie about being from Russia, to throw people off her trail. *She's craftier than I had previously believed,* he thought.

Just then, the waitress came over. "Here's your cheeseburger and fries, with extra gravy, ketchup, and mustard," she said, grimacing. "Can I get you anything?" she asked Weasel, who was gazing amazedly at Manya's delicious concoction. It was exactly what he often ordered for himself!

The waitress cleared her throat in an annoyed way.

"Oh, yes," Weasel said, snapping to attention. "I'd like a can of cola. Shaken, not stirred," he added, James Bond style.

"You want me to shake your can of soda?" She raised her eyebrows.

"That's what I said," Weasel said, narrowing his eyes.

She shrugged and left.

"So . . . uh . . . You go to Bayside High School, where I go," Manya said.

"Me? In high school? Ha-ha-ha!" Weasel laughed broadly. "I'm a businessman," he said, suddenly serious. "I'm in international sales." He leaned across the table, putting his face up close to Manya's. "Do *you* have anything of an international nature you'd like to sell?" he asked.

Manya looked confused. "I don't think so," she answered.

Yep, she sure denied that fast, Weasel thought. *She must be guilty, or she wouldn't have been so quick to answer. I'm definitely right: She's a Soviet spy!*

Just then the waitress came back with his soda. "Okay, I shook it for you," she said, and walked away.

Weasel winked at Manya and popped the top of the

can. *Fzzzt!* Cola squirted all over his face and the table.

"Oh!" Manya squealed. "You made a mess!"

Weasel coolly wiped brown fizz from his face. "Don't worry, sweetheart. It'll all come out in the wash."

Manya looked at him curiously again.

"Oh, look!" Weasel pointed at the door of the Max, over Manya's right shoulder. "It's Shaquille O'Neal!"

Manya turned around to look. She didn't know who he was talking about, but he sounded excited. When she didn't see anyone unusual, she turned around again to ask him what he was talking about. But no one was sitting across from her.

Special Agent Weazemeister had vanished once again.

chapter

7

On Wednesday, Scott sat in study hall, his notebook open in front of him. All the horoscopes were
written except Taurus—Dave Williams's sign. Scott
was desperately trying to come up with some advice
that would convince Dave to ask Vicki to the dance.

He sighed and looked around the quiet classroom.
The other students were bent over their desks, working on homework or reading. He noticed that the front
seat of the middle row was still empty. At least Bruce
McKeone had taken *his* horoscope advice—he was so
scared of getting sick that he had stayed home all
week. He and Vicki wouldn't be going to the dance
together, but Dave was still a problem.

Scott put his head down on his desk in frustration. A second later, he sat bolt upright. "I've got it!" he practically shouted. As his words echoed in the quiet room, everyone turned around and stared at him.

"Is there something wrong, Mr. Ericson?" the teacher asked. "Do I need to remind you that study hall is for quiet study?"

"There's nothing wrong at all, Mrs. Healy," Scott said, picking up his pen and starting to write. "In fact, I think everything's just perfect."

o   o   o

"Megan! Wait up!"

Megan turned around to see Vicki running toward her. She started to say hi, but Vicki interrupted.

"You've got to help me with this big story," she said, excitedly grabbing Megan's arm.

"It's going to be tough to help you with your fingernails embedded in my flesh," Megan replied, wincing.

"Oh. Sorry." Vicki released her grip. "But I really need you to help me. My last story was so killer, and this one has to be even better!"

"Vicki, I'd like to help you, but I'm supposed to go to French Club," Megan explained.

"Excuse me? French Club?" Vicki put a hand on her hip and raised her eyebrows.

"Yeah, French Club," Megan responded, wondering what Vicki's problem was.

"Well, that's *très* interesting, but I think Lindsay said you were supposed to help me with my article," Vicki said snottily.

"Whoa," Megan said. Vicki sure was getting an attitude about her newspaper assignments!

Then again, she reflected, she *had* offered to help. Maybe French Club could do without her for a day.

"Okay," she agreed. "So what's your idea for this big story?"

"The school's janitors. They're supposed to clean the school, but look what I found!" Vicki held up a small plastic bag that was full of some kind of brownish black muck.

"Gross; what *is* that?" Megan wrinkled her nose.

"I don't know," Vicki said darkly, "but it was caked in the crevices between the tiles in the basement. And I do mean *caked*. I picked this stuff out with an old toothbrush. The custodial staff is supposed to clean this stuff off of the floor!"

In the basement? Megan thought. *Did anyone really go around scrubbing the basement tiles with a toothbrush?* "Um, Vicki," she said. "Does anyone really care if there's a little dirt between the tiles in the basement?"

"Whether people care isn't my problem," Vicki announced. "I care!"

"Well, a little dirt on the floor won't kill anyone." Megan shrugged. "Especially if it's in a place where no one spends a whole lot of time."

"Are you sure about that?" Vicki asked, narrowing her eyes. "That's how diseases get spread around, you know. A little dirt here and there, and the next thing you know, we'll all be infected!"

Megan tried again, "But Vicki—"

"Come on, we can't waste any time!" Vicki ignored Megan's protests and dragged her into the *Beacon* office.

Three hours later, they were still working on the article. Vicki had a clipboard and a pencil in hand, and Megan had a pile of plastic bags, some stickers, and a pencil sharpener.

"Okay," Vicki said commandingly. "Bag number eighteen!"

"Eighteen," Megan said wearily as she pulled the bag marked with that number out of the pile.

"Bag number eighteen is from the top of the lockers on the third floor. I collected it yesterday after school," Vicki said, checking her clipboard. "What does the material look like?"

"It looks like dust, and maybe some lint," Megan said, poking listlessly at the bag.

"Ah-ha! Dust contains airborne toxins. That amount of dust must have been building up for months! I'll bet those lockers haven't been cleaned since last spring!"

Vicki began writing down her observations, but her pencil lead broke.

"Oh, here, sharpen this one, will you?" Vicki tossed the pencil over to Megan and pulled another one out of her bookbag.

Megan gritted her teeth and sharpened the pencil. She was starting to get a little steamed about the way Vicki was treating her. *I didn't sign on as chief pencil sharpener!* she thought.

But more than that, Megan was tired of Vicki's big scoop. She felt like she had been sitting there for years, and she didn't see what the point was. Where did Vicki find the time to scrape gunk out of every corner of the school?

"All right," Vicki continued. "Now on to bag number nineteen."

"Vicki, can we talk for a second?"

"Megan, don't get me wrong, but this story is very important. We really have to keep working."

"That's what I want to talk about. Are you sure this story is a good idea?"

Vicki put her pencil down and looked up at her friend.

74

Megan took a deep breath and continued. "It's just that—well—I noticed that everyone got really mad at the cafeteria ladies after reading your story, and I heard that they got in trouble with Mr. Belding."

"Well, you read the story. The conditions were disgusting!"

"They weren't *that* bad. And besides, the cafeteria ladies can only do what the school superintendent tells them to do. It's not their fault, but they got blamed!"

"So what, Megan?" Vicki was looking really annoyed. "When the system fails, somebody's got to take the fall."

"I just don't think that what you're doing is fair," Megan argued. "I mean, these people's jobs are on the line. They could get fired if you keep writing these stories."

"Oh, great—so what are we supposed to do? Leave everything gross and disgusting so we can protect some people's jobs?"

"Vicki, Bayside's not perfect, but it's definitely not gross and disgusting."

"Well, it's gross and disgusting by my standards," Vicki retorted.

That was it. Megan had been really patient over the last few hours because this story seemed to mean so much to Vicki. But enough was enough! Vicki was driving her nuts!

"Vicki, you are ridiculous. *No one* could live up to your standards. You could walk into an antiseptic operating room and find a dust bunny! You would complain about dust in a space shuttle!"

"Oh, really?" Vicki stood up and put her hands on her hips.

"Yes, really!" Megan yelled. "I don't care if there's a little dirt on the floor. And I think your story is irresponsible and stupid!"

"Well!" Vicki's cheeks turned pink with anger. She crossed her arms. "So the ugly truth finally comes out. You know, Megan, I wouldn't expect you to understand. You don't know anything about journalism. I am committed to my job on this paper; and you know what? I think you're just jealous because my great story got so much attention!"

"Jealous? *Jealous? Ha!*" Megan shouted. She picked up one of Vicki's pencils and snapped it in half.

"Hey, those are made with special hypoallergenic graphite. Leave them alone!" Vicki shouted.

"You think I'm jealous of you?" Megan answered, breaking another pencil. "I was glad that your story was such a hit. But that doesn't make you the queen of Bayside!"

"And what is that supposed to mean?" Vicki asked, grabbing the rest of her pencils.

76

"It means I don't remember Lindsay making me the pencil-sharpening editor or the sludge clerk of the *Bayside Beacon!*" Megan took all thirty plastic bags and dropped them out the window.

"*My research!*" Vicki shrieked as she ran to the window. "You dropped it all into the dumpster!"

"Needleman, the dumpster is exactly where your dumb 'news scoop' belongs," Megan said. Then she stalked out the door.

chapter

8

The next day was Thursday, which left only one more day to get out the special edition of the *Bayside Beacon*! Weasel powered up the bank of computers in the newspaper office and got his army of electronic wizards to work. He was feeling a little nervous. He had been spending so much time spying on Manya that he had neglected his duties on the newspaper.

He sat down at the biggest computer, at the end of the row. When he turned it on, it beeped, telling him that he had some messages on his computer-network bulletin board. He logged on and began to read.

Suddenly he yelped and leaped out of his chair. His five assistants looked over at him.

"Mr. Weasel? Are you okay?" Jennifer asked.

"What? Okay? Sure, I'm okay! Why—don't you think I'm okay?"

Jennifer took her hands off the keyboard and adjusted her glasses. "Well, you did just jump up as if a shark had bitten you," she said.

"Oh! I was just . . . um . . . My foot fell asleep. Nothing to be alarmed about." Weasel began hopping up and down, slapping his right leg. "See? I can feel sensation returning right now. Ha-ha. Nothing to be suspicious of."

The five computer hackers looked at him quizzically, and Weasel stopped hopping.

"Okay, back to work," he said, cracking his knuckles.

Jennifer shook her head and returned to work. The rest of them followed suit.

Weasel breathed a sigh of relief and sat down at his computer again. He reread the message that had scared him so badly.

"CCCP," his computer screen read. "Sorry! I had a problem with my key. But you know who you are. And I think maybe you know how I feel about you, too."

CCCP? It was another message from the Russian spy! But what did it mean? Weasel read it again.

"I had a problem with my key." Weasel peered over

at his fellow computer hackers. They were all typing away, not noticing him at all. He looked back at his screen.

A key. That can only mean the solution to a secret code, he thought. *So the Russian spy is writing in code! I've got to figure out what this message means in code!*

Weasel cracked his knuckles again. The best way to get anything done was with the right program, he knew. All he needed to do was to get the computer to crack the code for him! He began typing furiously.

Soon he had four separate programs running at the same time, working to crack the code. He crossed his arms, sat back, and waited.

o o o

"Okay, Lindsay! I've got my article for the paper," Tommy announced as he walked into the *Beacon* office later that day.

Lindsay looked up from the article she was editing and smiled wanly. Her dark hair was hanging down around her face, and she had shadows under her eyes.

"That's great, Tommy!" she said, kissing him hello.

"Uh-oh," Tommy said, sitting next to her at the table. "You look beat."

"I guess I am, sort of," Lindsay admitted. She pulled her hair back into a loose ponytail and wrapped a bright, fabric-covered hair tie around it.

"Well, what's up, babe?" Tommy asked, tugging on her ponytail.

"Well, I just talked to Megan. She had a huge fight with Vicki over the article they're working on. It looks like Vicki is taking this newspaper assignment way too seriously," she explained with a sigh. "Those two never fight. And I feel like it's my fault."

"Why?" Tommy asked.

"Well, I'm in charge here," Lindsay replied wearily. "The paper is my responsibility."

"That doesn't mean that their argument is your fault, Lindsay," Tommy said soothingly. "But I guess I can understand how you feel."

"Well, at least you did your article," Lindsay said, brightening. "So you're not upset about how people reacted to the last one?"

"Hey, I've been improving my writing skills," Tommy answered. He pulled a notebook out and plopped it onto the table in front of her.

"That's great," Lindsay said, kissing the tip of her boyfriend's nose. "I wish everyone else had an attitude like yours. Okay, let me take a look."

Smiling, Lindsay began to scan the first paragraph. But as she read on, her smile faded.

"Pretty great, right?" Tommy said, giving her a little punch on the arm. She looked up at him and looked back at the notebook, not saying anything.

"Lindsay?" he said. "Don't you like it?"

Lindsay set the notebook down on the table and looked up at her boyfriend. "Tommy, what did you do to your writing?" she asked softly.

"I made it interesting. You said the first article was boring, so I made this one more exciting."

Lindsay picked the article up and began reading aloud. "'The football team frolicked at a remote site on Saturday. It was a strenuous game, but the stalwart lads of Bayside emerged victorious. Chief among the justifications for this result were the aggressive attacks mounted by the team members.' Tommy, what are you trying to say here?"

"Just that the football team played an away game on Saturday. It was a tough game, but we won. The offense played really good. I tried to jazz it up a little," Tommy explained. "Why, is there something wrong with it?"

"Wrong? Well, no, it's not *wrong*," Lindsay began. "It's just . . ."

82

"I can't believe it! You don't like it. You think it stinks!" Tommy stood up suddenly, knocking his chair backward.

"No, no, Tommy," Lindsay said quickly, "it's okay, it's just a little—"

"A little what? You're going to change it all around, aren't you?" he challenged her.

Lindsay looked distraught. "Well, I—"

"I should have known," Tommy said bitterly. "Nothing I do is good enough for you. Okay, go ahead; I don't care anymore. Do whatever you want to it."

"No! No, I'm not going to change it. Okay?" Lindsay stood up and handed Tommy the notebook. "I'm not changing a word. Just take it to Weasel, and he'll put it on the computer, okay?"

Tommy looked at the notebook. Finally, he took it from Lindsay. Without a word, he left the office.

Lindsay sat down at the table and sighed. First Megan and Vicki had gotten into a major fight. Now Tommy was hurt and angry. This newspaper job was turning her life into a nightmare!

o   o   o

Several hours later, Weasel sat alone in the *Beacon* office, staring at his computer screen. His eyes were bloodshot. His shirt was unbuttoned, and his hair was sticking straight up because he kept scratching his head. He had had to rewrite his decoding program six times, but he thought he had it right this time. He moved a shaky hand to the ENTER key and pushed. The computer hummed for a moment, then beeped. Weasel jumped. Words appeared on the screen.

"Message decoded," it said.

"Okay, okay, what does it say?" Weasel asked, tapping the keys again.

"Aliens invade the vestibule," the computer screen read. "Disembowel leader and continue scramlok."

Holy moley, Weasel thought, gripping the desk in front of him. *The aliens must mean the Soviet spies. They're going to invade our outer states, and kill someone by disembowelling him!* He paused for a second. *But what's a scramlok?* He looked in his dictionary, but he couldn't find a listing for the word.

Weasel looked back at the computer. *My decoding programs must be incomplete*, he thought. *I might not be able to crack the whole code, but I got most of it. This is really big!*

He sat back in his chair and stroked his chin. Weasel was the only one who knew what was going on, and it was up to him to stop it. And he already knew who the spy was: Manya! It had to be—she had acted so suspiciously when he questioned her at the Max.

Suddenly he remembered something else—the phone call he had overheard. Manya had mentioned that someone was coming from Russia, and she had said she planned to kill him! So that was the plan—to create an international incident, maybe even try to start a war! The questions were, who was Manya planning to kill, and where was she going to do it?

The fate of the nation rested on Weasel. He had to get to Manya and foil her plot, and he had to do it fast!

chapter 9

When Scott got to school on Friday morning, Bayside High was deserted. He had gotten there an hour early so that he could carry out his plan to get Vicki and Dave together.

He looked around, feeling a little silly. The only people he saw were a few people from the swim team, who had practice before school. But they were so groggy they didn't even notice him.

Scott yawned and stretched as he stood in the empty hallway. He looked around to make sure no one saw him. Then he went over to Dave Williams's locker and slipped a note into it.

"That ought to do it," Scott murmured as he poked the note through the vents. He heard it fall inside with a muffled plunk.

Satisfied, Scott yawned and stretched again. He had taken care of Vicki's love life; now it was time to concentrate on fixing up Megan. But first, he was going to stop off in the *Bayside Beacon* office for a little nap.

o   o   o

When Tommy D. walked into the cafeteria at lunchtime, he thought he heard someone snickering behind his back. He whipped around, but he only saw a couple of people reading the new edition of the *Beacon*, which had just come out. He scratched his head and kept walking.

A few moments later he set his tray down at a table where Lindsay, Scott, Megan, and Vicki were eating lunch. He thought he heard more snickering, so he glared down the table. The rest of the gang just looked back at him, so he looked at the next table. Some of his friends from the football team were there, and they all looked down when he turned around. They *were* laughing at him!

"What's so funny?" he asked.

The table was silent.

"Okay, whatever," Tommy said, turning his back to the football table and sitting down with his friends. He opened his milk. "Did anybody read my article in the paper?"

The guys at the next table erupted in laughter and started slapping one another on the back. One guy was laughing so hard that milk came out of his nose.

"Just ignore them," Lindsay said, squeezing Tommy's arm. Tommy stood up and turned to the next table, staring at his football friends. Usually his stare was so scary that he could make someone stop in his or her tracks with a single look. But right now everyone was laughing so hard that they didn't even notice Tommy's glare.

"What's so funny?" Tommy asked again. He grabbed the nearest person—Brian Saunders, the quarterback—and lifted him off his feet. "Would you like to tell me what is so funny?" he growled.

"Hey, Tommy, I'm sorry!" Brian still couldn't stop laughing, and by now tears were streaming out of his eyes. He held up a copy of the *Beacon* and waved it around. "It's just that—put me down, man—your article is really great. We all think it's really funny!"

"Funny?" Tommy D. let go of Brian, who dropped to the floor.

"You mean you weren't trying to be funny?" Brian asked, rubbing his shoulders. The rest of the table had stopped laughing.

Tommy picked up a copy of the paper and started to read his article again. All of a sudden, he saw what they were talking about. He had used all those big words in the article so that he would sound smarter, but none of them made any sense. The whole article just sounded stupid!

"Oh, yeah, man, it was all a joke," he told Brian, trying to sound lighthearted. "Glad you liked it."

Brian's face lost its anxious look. "Great stuff, Mr. D.," he said. "I especially loved the bit about 'frolicking in a remote location.' It was brilliant!" He burst out laughing again.

Tommy put the paper down next to his lunch and sat down. But for some reason, he didn't feel like eating.

Megan turned the newspaper over, so that Tommy's article wasn't showing, and smoothed it out. "Tommy?" she said, trying to get his attention. But he just stared at his hands, looking glum. She glanced down at the newspaper, trying to think of something else to catch his attention. The paper was open to the horoscopes.

"Hey, look, Tommy, your horoscope," she said brightly. "Don't you want to read it?" She tossed a grin at Scott. "You know, 'Madame Moussaka' has been making some pretty accurate predictions lately."

Tommy picked up the paper again. "Taurus," he read. "Someone's going to give you advice that you didn't ask for. You might not have thought of it before, but you should listen to it!" He put the paper down and glowered. "I'm going to be getting a lot of advice about my writing," he grumbled. "Maybe I should take it, and quit writing for the paper."

Scott sat up, startled. "I didn't know you were a Taurus, Tommy," he said. "You know, you really shouldn't take the horoscopes so seriously. I mean, what's good advice to one person may not be good advice for someone else!"

"What are you talking about, Scott?" Tommy growled. "Never mind. I don't understand anything. I'll catch you guys later."

"Tommy—" Lindsay called out, but Tommy was already heading for the door.

Megan put a hand on her arm. "I think he just wants to be alone," she told Lindsay. Lindsay slumped back in her seat and frowned.

"I feel so awful," she said. "Nothing is going right with this dumb paper!"

"Are you kidding me?" Scott asked. "The paper is great! Even Mr. Belding thinks so." He stood up and went to get another carton of milk.

"Lindsay, you're doing a *great* job with the paper," Vicki assured her.

"Well, so the paper's a success, but my life is a mess," Lindsay said, leaning her chin in her hand. "I wanted to encourage Tommy to use his sports knowledge to write for the paper, but the fact is, he hates writing. And when I tried to edit him, I hurt his feelings. But when I left his article the way it was, people made fun of him, and it hurt his feelings more. I feel like I can't do anything right. This paper is ruining my whole life!"

"Hey, Lindsay, with me as your star reporter, you've got nothing to worry about," Vicki announced brightly.

Megan snorted.

"What's your problem?" Vicki turned to Megan.

"I don't have a problem," Megan replied innocently. "I'm just wondering who's going to sharpen your pencils and sort out your little plastic bags while you're busy being the star reporter."

"Well, I don't know, Megan," Vicki said in a syrupy-sweet voice. "But whoever it is, I'm sure they'll be more mature and less jealous than you."

91

"Oh, right!" Megan snapped. "There you go again, telling me I'm jealous of you. What makes you think I'm jealous, anyway?"

"You must be," Vicki answered her. "I wrote the lead story, and it got all that attention. You hardly wrote anything!"

"Hey, wait, you guys—" Lindsay tried to interrupt, but the argument was heating up.

"Please! That is the most ridiculous thing I've ever heard," Megan responded. "I don't care if you win the Pulitzer Prize, Vicki! The truth is that you're acting like a snotty little jerk about your newspaper stories!"

"You know, Megan, you're really getting on my nerves," Vicki said. "I don't care if we never work together again!"

"Guys!" Lindsay yelled. "Please don't fight, okay? You're supposed to be friends!"

Megan was silent for a moment. She didn't want to lose her temper again, so she picked up her milk. But a second later she put it down. She was just too angry! "Ah—Ah—*Achoo!*" she yelled, pretending to sneeze on Vicki's granola bar.

"Oh, *gross!*" Vicki stood up. "That's *it*, Megan. You've gone too far!"

"Hey, guys," Scott interrupted as he came back to the table, "what's going on?"

"I guess I'm just jealous," Megan said to Vicki, ignoring Scott. She smiled primly. "Aren't you going to say 'Bless you'?"

"Bless you," Vicki grumbled. She and Megan sat stiffly next to each other.

"This is exactly what I mean," Lindsay said. "The newspaper is making us all crazy. You guys are fighting, and it's all because of the *Bayside Beacon*!" Her eyes filled with tears. "Ever since I revived this stupid paper, everything has just gone totally wrong."

"Oh, Lindsay, don't feel so bad. We're not fighting," Vicki said. "Megan's just being jealous. She even admitted it!"

"Can it, Needleman," Megan said.

"See?" Vicki put her hands out. "I can't win . . . I forgot to get a straw. Does anyone else want something?"

No one said anything. Vicki shrugged, got up from her seat, and went to the front of the cafeteria. Lindsay picked at her food. Everyone was feeling rotten.

Everyone except Scott. His heart leaped up when he saw Dave Williams talking to Vicki. Dave was holding a piece of paper—a note—in his hand, and he glanced at it hesitantly as he chatted with Vicki. After a while, he leaned close to her and whispered something in her ear. Vicki blushed and nodded.

As Dave walked away, Vicki rushed back to Megan, Scott, and Lindsay, forgetting her straw completely. "You guys, guess what!" she crowed.

"You just got hired by the *National Enquirer*?" Megan asked sarcastically.

"No, for real; guess what? I have a date for the Halloween dance!" Vicki announced.

"No way! Who?" Lindsay asked.

"Dave Williams. The guy who saved Homer's life!" Vicki sang. "He just asked me. He's awfully cute, and he *is* going to be a doctor. What could be better?"

"That's awesome, Vicki," Scott said. He was ecstatic. His plan had worked!

"I'm so excited," Vicki said, picking up her granola bar. "I kind of hoped I would go with Bruce. But he's been out sick, and I don't think he can go, so I was desperate for a date!"

Scott looked proudly over at Lindsay. Now she would understand what he'd been up to! She'd see that his scheming and scamming could do *good* things for his friends.

But Lindsay wasn't looking at Scott. Her eyes were

focused on someone else. Scott followed her gaze to Megan's stricken face.

Uh-oh, he thought with a sinking feeling. *Is there something going on here I don't know about?*

chapter

10
—

Megan sat at the table for a few minutes, looking hurt. Then she quietly got up and left. Lindsay watched her go, but she didn't get up and follow her.

Vicki was so excited about her date that she didn't even notice. She just chattered about the dance while she finished her lunch. Finally, Vicki finished the last of her organic yogurt and popped the container into her empty lunch bag. "Well!" she announced as she stood up to leave. "I've had an awesome lunch, but it's time to get back to work. I've got a lot of research to do for my next big story!"

Now that he and Lindsay were alone at the table,

Scott leaned forward. "Are you going to tell me what's going on?" he asked Lindsay in a low voice.

Lindsay looked back at him, obviously torn. "I promised I wouldn't," she said.

"Come on, it's obvious something's up," Scott pressed.

Lindsay nodded slowly. "It's just that . . . well . . . Megan kind of has a crush on Dave. She's actually liked him for a long time, but you know how she is. She doesn't like to make a big fuss over boys and stuff like that."

"Megan likes Dave?" Scott was dumbfounded. That possibility had never even occurred to him!

"Yeah. Vicki doesn't know, but Megan and Vicki are so mad at each other lately! This is definitely not going to help improve things between them."

"Oh, man." Scott put his head down on the table. "Oh, *man.*"

"Scott, it's a bummer, but it's not *that* bad," Lindsay said.

"Yes, it is!" Scott wailed, lifting his head and shaking back his brown hair.

"What is it? What's wrong?" Lindsay asked.

Scott didn't answer.

Lindsay looked closely at him, suspicion blooming

in her eyes. "Scott Ericson, what have you been up to?" she demanded.

"It's me. I got Dave to go out with Vicki instead of Megan!"

While Lindsay frowned at him, Scott explained how he had been using the horoscopes to match Dave and Vicki up.

"But I don't get it," Lindsay said. "If Dave didn't believe his horoscope the first time, how did you get him to believe it the second time?"

"I stuck an anonymous note in his locker, telling him that he had to ask Vicki to the dance. And I wrote the Taurus horoscope, telling him to listen to any advice he gets!"

"And the coincidence—the anonymous note plus the horoscope—was just too much to ignore," Lindsay said, nodding her head. "I have to admit, it's a brilliant plan."

"And it worked!" Scott boasted, in spite of himself.

"Yeah, *great*, Scott." Lindsay yanked Scott back to reality. "Meanwhile, Megan is heartbroken, and Vicki has no idea that anything is wrong, and it's all because of another one of your schemes," she pointed out.

"But I didn't know!" Scott groaned. "I thought I had it all figured out!"

"Well, I hate to say I told you so—" Lindsay began.

"No, you don't," Scott objected. "You *love* to say 'I told you so.'" He hung his head. "And you're right. You warned me not to mess in other people's business."

"Well, yeah, I did." Lindsay and Scott both laughed. "So what are you going to do about it?" she asked.

"I'm not sure," Scott replied. "But I'd better get started." He looked up at Lindsay. "I don't know how you do it."

"How I do what?"

"How you keep everything so together," Scott said, smiling. "I mean, I make all these plans, and it always gets screwed up. But you always seem to have everything under control." He shook his head. "Thanks for the advice, Lindsay. I'll see you later." He hurried out of the cafeteria.

I have everything under control? Lindsay thought. *He's got to be kidding me. I've messed up everything lately!*

Shaking her head, Lindsay left the cafeteria and headed over to the bleachers by the football field. Nobody was around. The sky was overcast, and everything looked gloomy. Tommy was sitting by himself near the top of the bleachers.

"I had a feeling I'd find you here," Lindsay said, sitting next to him.

Tommy just sat there, huddled in his football jacket and staring at his feet.

"Tommy, don't you want to talk to me at all?" Lindsay asked.

"What am I supposed to say?" he mumbled.

"You can say, 'Lindsay, I'm really steamed at you,'" Lindsay offered.

"But I'm not steamed at you," Tommy objected, finally looking up. "I'm steamed at myself. I feel like I let you down."

"No! You did the best you could do. That's all I wanted," Lindsay said.

"But I really wanted to write a great article by myself," Tommy explained. "You were working so hard on the paper, and I knew it was stressing you out."

"Oh, Tommy!" Lindsay put her arms around her boyfriend's neck and kissed his cheek. "I *was* really stressed out, and I pushed you way too hard! Don't write for the paper anymore if you don't want to."

"I don't know." Tommy sighed. "Maybe you should be with a brainier guy than me. Maybe Scott Ericson would be a better match for you."

"What?" Lindsay whacked Tommy on the arm. "Don't even think that, Tommy D. Scott is a fun guy, and he's a good friend, but *you're* the one for me. I love you just the way you are. Okay?"

"Okay." Tommy sounded relieved. "But I still think I let you down. You kept wanting to change everything I wrote."

"Tommy, that's what editors *do*. They change everything around because they're in charge of how it sounds. It's not an attack on *you*. It's just how newspaper writing works. Everybody gets edited."

"Really?" Tommy asked.

"Really."

"Oh." Tommy thought for a minute. "Well, I guess I could keep writing for the paper. If you really want me to," he added dubiously. It was obvious that he had had enough of being a staff writer.

"Tommy, you've been really great. I know writing for the newspaper is the last thing you want to do. And I'm sorry for making you do it in the first place. It's totally fine with me if you want to stop doing it."

They sat quietly for a few minutes.

"I'll tell you what," Tommy said softly as he wrapped a lock of Lindsay's hair around his finger. "I already started my next article, on the soccer team. I'll finish that one, and you can do whatever you want with it. And then my newspaper career is over."

Lindsay smiled up at Tommy. He really was a great

guy. "Perfect," she agreed. "That will give me time to find someone to replace you on the paper."

Tommy nodded, grinning.

"So is everything okay now?" Lindsay asked, leaning forward.

Tommy leaned over and gave her a soft, warm kiss. "Yeah," he said. "Everything is just great."

11

When school let out on Friday, Megan walked through the gray drizzle to the Max. The whole gang usually met there. But today Megan was feeling a little nervous. She and Vicki still weren't speaking to each other, and Megan was afraid that if their other friends weren't around, she and Vicki would either sit there feeling uncomfortable, or have another big fight. Neither option made her very happy.

Megan didn't want to fight with Vicki anymore. Life was pretty lonely without a best friend. But Vicki was so busy being star reporter that she didn't even notice she was treating Megan like an idiot. And as if that wasn't bad enough, Vicki was going to the dance with Dave Williams!

Of course, Megan reminded herself, Vicki didn't know that Megan liked Dave. Megan had kept her crush secret. But that didn't make Megan feel any better. She was still so jealous that she thought she would scream.

Maybe I should walk around for a while, Megan thought when she reached the door of the Max. *Then there'll be a better chance that Vicki won't be in there alone.* Then she shook her head. *Don't be such a coward, Megan*, she told herself. She took a deep breath and went in.

Sure enough, Vicki was sitting alone at their usual table. Megan's heart fell, but she walked up to the table and sat down. Vicki looked up, and Megan could see that she was holding a copy of the *Beacon*. She looked kind of bummed.

"Uh . . . is everything okay?" Megan asked.

"Nothing's okay," Vicki answered. "You should know that better than anyone!"

"What do you mean?" Megan looked at the paper. The article about the custodial staff was splashed across the front of the paper, just like the cafeteria article.

104

"Everyone loved my first article," Vicki lamented. "But they're hardly paying any attention to this one. What's the matter with it?"

"Well, let's take a look at it," Megan said. She half expected Vicki to bite her head off, but Vicki just slid the paper across the table so that Megan could see it.

The headline, in big block letters, said, JANITOR SCANDAL: THE HEALTH OF BAYSIDE STUDENTS IS AT RISK BECAUSE OF NEGLIGENCE!

"That's kind of a harsh way of making your point," Megan pointed out.

"I guess," Vicki said, squinting at the page. "But it's true! I really think that the school should be kept cleaner."

"Vicki, I kind of lost my temper the other day, and I'm sorry about that. But what I was saying is still true! Other people don't feel the same way you do about how clean everything has to be!"

"Yeah, maybe," Vicki agreed reluctantly. "But that doesn't make it okay for the school to be so gross!"

"Be realistic," Megan said. "Look. In your article, you demand hypoallergenic paper towels in all the bathrooms. There's no way the school is going to do that! It's too expensive, and it's honestly not necessary!"

"Maybe my standards are a little too high for other people," Vicki admitted sheepishly. "But it didn't bother them when I was writing about the cafeteria!"

"Well, everyone hates the cafeteria food already. It was an easy target! But everybody really likes Mr. Monza, the custodian," Megan pointed out. "Okay, so there's slime in the basement and dust on top of the lockers. It's not because he's goofing off! He does the best job he can. And also, he's a really good guy. Don't you remember that weekend when you needed your asthma medication, and he unlocked all the classrooms until you found it?"

"I forgot all about that!" Vicki said, her eyes widening.

Megan thought she might finally be getting through to her friend. "And remember when Weasel left his box of computer disks in Mr. Belding's office, and he was too scared to go in there and get it? Mr. Monza went in, told Mr. Belding he had to wash his windows, and got Weasel's disks for him."

"I forgot about that, too," Vicki said glumly. "I guess there's a lot more to Mr. Monza than just how well he scrubs the floor."

"Not to mention the fact that there's just him and one assistant cleaning the whole school by themselves," Megan continued. "That's a lot of work for two people."

"Ugh," Vicki groaned as she put her head in her hands. "I got so caught up in my investigation that I totally forgot that there was another side to the story." She put her hands back down on the table and frowned. After a second she looked at her friend.

"You're right, Megan," she said, her cheeks turning pink. "And—and thanks for explaining it to me. I'm going to have to print an apology in next week's newspaper."

"To Mr. Monza?" Megan asked.

"Yeah, to Mr. Monza. But while I'm at it, I should really print one to you, too."

"Oh, really?" Megan said teasingly. "Why would you want to do that?"

"I was horrible to you. I was so sure I was doing the right thing, I got totally carried away. I forgot that you're my friend!"

"Well, you *were* a little difficult," Megan agreed. She smiled and drummed her fingers on the table. This apology was getting better and better, and she was enjoying it!

"I was impossible!" Vicki persisted. "I can't believe you're even speaking to me!"

"Me neither." Megan was impressed.

"I'm the worst person in the world!" Vicki wailed.

"Yep, pretty much," Megan said again.

"Well, you don't have to be *that* agreeable," Vicki protested.

Megan laughed. "Okay, okay," she said. "It's water under the bridge. No harm done—*if* you promise to print that apology and to be more responsible about your choice of articles in the future. All right?"

"All right," Vicki agreed. "I really am sorry, Megan."

"It's cool," Megan said. She still felt kind of bad about Dave, but she didn't know how to bring it up or what to say. Fortunately, she looked up and saw Scott coming into the Max.

"Hey, Scott!" she yelled, waving to him. "Where have you been?"

Scott came up to the table. "I've been busy," he explained. "Hey Vicki, can I talk to you alone?"

"Whoops, that's my cue," Megan said, relieved. "I'm going to go sit with my study partners." She crossed the Max and sat with some girls from her Biology class.

Vicki looked at Scott quizzically as he slid into the seat across from her. Bruce and Dave were all of a sudden interested in her—was Scott finally going to get interested, too?

108

"What's up, Scott?" she asked.

"Vicki, I have a horrible confession to make," Scott said. "And I've been running around all day today, trying to fix it up, but you're the one who deserves an apology the most."

Vicki stared at Scott, wide-eyed, while he told her all about his plans to use the horoscope as a matchmaker.

"So I called Bruce already," Scott continued. "And I told him what I did, so he knows he doesn't really have to stay home. And then I tracked Dave down and explained it all to him, too."

"But what about my date for the Halloween dance?" Vicki exclaimed, her voice full of panic.

"That's the worst part," Scott said. "See, I didn't realize this, but Megan really has a thing for Dave."

Vicki gasped. No wonder Megan was so unhappy! "Oh, no!" she said. "Oh, I can't go to the dance with him, then. I don't like him *that* much!"

"Really?" Scott was relieved. "So you don't mind?"

"Scott, how could I be mad at you for this?" she said, laughing. "You were just trying to be a good friend. Thanks for trying to fix me up!" She leaned closer and batted her eyelashes. "You sure went to a lot of trouble. Maybe you really do care, huh, Scottie?" she asked teasingly.

Scott leaned back, alarmed. Was Vicki still head over heels for him?

"Uh—look! Here's Dave. I think you guys should talk." Scott left the table abruptly.

Vicki looked up and saw Dave Williams walking toward her table. Across the Max, she saw Megan gazing wistfully at him. Vicki smiled.

"Vicki, we—I—um—I have to tell you something," Dave said nervously as he approached the table.

"Sit down, Dave," Vicki said. "Scott told me everything. It's cool. You don't have to go to the dance with me."

Dave looked relieved as he sank into the seat across from Vicki.

"And if you'll excuse me," Vicki went on, "I think there's someone else you need to talk to." She stood up and motioned for Megan to come over.

Megan looked confused, but she came and sat in Vicki's seat. Vicki walked over to where Scott was standing, by the door of the Max, and watched as Dave and Megan talked intensely, then laughed. Finally Dave said something to Megan, and Megan nodded, beaming.

"Ah, young love," Vicki said. "It almost makes my tear ducts unclog."

"Hey, Vicki," a voice behind them called. Vicki and Scott turned around. Bruce McKeone was walking toward them.

"Bruce!" Vicki exclaimed. "What are you doing here? I thought you were allergic to the air-conditioning they use in the Max."

"I am. But I had to see you," Bruce explained, sniffling. "I need to ask you something."

Scott winked at Bruce as he left the Max. He felt great. It hadn't happened exactly as he had expected, but he had found dates for the Halloween dance for all his friends! All his friends except Weasel, that was.

Hey, he thought. *Where is Weasel, anyway?*

chapter

12

"Wow! The walls in the ladies' room are pink!" Weasel exclaimed, admiring the lovely decor surrounding him. Then he remembered: This was not a pleasure trip. He was here on serious business.

Weasel was in the Palisades Chamber of Commerce. He had just shimmied in through a small window, since no self-respecting spy could be seen walking in through the front door during an undercover operation.

Unfortunately, the window had proved to open into the ladies' room. Fortunately, the room was deserted. Weasel stuck his head out the door and looked around. No one was in sight. He took off his trench

112

coat—it was soaked from the drizzly rain outside—
and put it in his backpack. Then he pulled his spy hat
further down on his forehead and crept out the door.

Weasel looked at the map he had drawn for himself. There was a group of Russian diplomats in the
building today, and he was sure that the Bayside spy—
Manya—was going to try to create an international
incident by assassinating one of them. He had figured
out where they would be, and now he prowled along
the hallway until he heard the murmuring sounds of a
meeting in the gigantic lobby of the building.

Sure enough, when he came around the corner of
the lobby, he saw the mayor of Bayside and several
portly men in three-piece suits standing on a platform.
In front of them were a bunch of reporters and photog-
raphers, asking questions about the men's visit to
California.

Weasel looked at everyone in the crowd carefully.
Then he spotted Manya! She was standing all the way
in the back, behind all the other people. She was wearing her crimson beret and scarf, and a bulky trench
coat.

"Ah-ha," Weasel whispered to himself. "A trench
coat. The fashion must of every secret agent. She's definitely a spy!"

He sidled up behind Manya. Just as the Russians

were exiting the room, he threw his arms around her and pulled her back into a hallway. She gasped and struggled, but Weasel gritted his teeth and held on.

"I know what you're up to. But you mustn't kill for the CCC—oof!" Weasel groaned as Manya elbowed him in the gut. He dropped to the floor, whimpering.

"Weasel!" Manya exclaimed. "Oh, I didn't know it was you!" She knelt down on the floor next to him.

He sat up, still unable to speak.

"Oh, I am so embarrassed," she said, blushing. Her accent was even thicker than usual because she was flustered. "You came all the way down here to find me and talk to me? That is so wonderful! Because I like you, too. I guess you figured out that I was sending you those messages on the computer. I just didn't expect you to be so—direct!"

Weasel was dumbfounded. First of all, he had never heard shy little Manya speak so much all at once. And second, what the heck was she talking about? She was supposed to be a spy!

"Messages—what do you mean?" Weasel finally squeaked out.

"You know. On the computer! I sent you the messages addressed to CP. You know, for *computer programmer*. Because you like to be hacking the computer all the time!"

"*CP?* But it said *CCCP!*" Weasel said.

"Yes; my computer is always sticking its keys," she said. "It came out like that. Remember, in the second message I told you I had trouble with my computer key?"

Weasel slapped himself in the head. "Then you're not a Soviet spy bent on destroying Western civilization as we know it?" he asked.

Now it was Manya's turn to be dumbfounded. "What is this you are saying?" she demanded, crossing her legs on the floor and knitting her brow.

"When I saw those messages to CCCP and everything, I thought there was secret spy activity going on. I thought you were a KGB agent, sent by the Soviet government to infiltrate Palisades. And I thought you were going to assassinate one of these Russian guys!"

Manya's big brown eyes got even bigger. She sat up straight. "Me? In the KGB? I hate the KGB!" Then she stopped, confused. "I was here because my uncle is one of the visiting Russians. I was supposed to meet him after the press conference. Did you think I was going to assassinate my uncle Vanya?"

"But I *heard* you. On the phone at school! You made sure he didn't know you were here. Then you said you were going to kill him!"

"Weasel! You have a big imagination. I was angry

because I thought he would go away without visiting me! Then I came here to surprise him." She laughed and shook her head. "You are very silly, Weasel."

"Your uncle Vanya. I can't believe it!" Weasel clapped his hand to his head. Maybe he *had* read too many spy novels!

o o o

By the next Saturday night, the Halloween Dance Committee had transformed the Bayside gym into a beautiful autumn ballroom. The lights were dimmed, and colored crepe paper was hanging across the ceiling. There were round tables arranged near the walls. Each table had a tablecloth, a centerpiece with orange flowers and little pumpkins, and pitchers of punch.

The *Beacon* gang sat down at their table. Everyone was in costume. Lindsay was with Tommy, of course. They were dressed as Romeo and Juliet. Megan and Dave sat next to them, in hospital scrubs and with stethoscopes around their necks. The bright blue of her cotton outfit set off Megan's dark skin; she looked radiant. Vicki and Bruce sat on the other side. They were both wearing strange-looking outfits with long, rubber spikes sticking out.

"Hey, Vicki, what are you guys supposed to be?"

Lindsay asked, adjusting her long, romantic white dress.

"We're pollen spores," Vicki explained. "That's what gets caught in your sinuses and gives you allergies."

"Oh! That's . . . interesting," Lindsay said brightly.

Suddenly, Vicki sneezed. Bruce stood up and moved the flower centerpiece away from her.

"Thanks, Bruce," Vicki said, smiling at him adoringly.

"Real flowers! I knew they'd cause trouble," he said, returning to her side.

Weasel came running up to the table. He was dressed in his super-duper spy outfit—only this time, it was just his Halloween costume.

"Folks, prepare to meet my date. The dashing and dangerous secret agent Manya!" Everyone looked up to see the shy, quiet, pretty girl—and did a double-take. Manya was wearing a crimson satin dress, off the shoulders, with a rhinestone necklace. Her face was flushed with excitement.

"Do you think I overdress?" she asked.

"No!" Scott said, standing. "You look—ravishing!"

"Hands off, Ericson," Weasel said, taking Manya by the arm. "Stick to your own date. Hey, where *is* your date?"

Everyone turned to look at Scott, who was dressed like a gangster in a pinstriped suit and hat.

He shrugged. "I guess I was so busy fixing everyone else up, I forgot about my own love life," he said sheepishly.

Just then, Rebecca Morrison, the head of the Bayside Drama Club, walked by. She was dressed all in black, like a Spanish dancer, and her red hair tumbled down her back. She tossed her head dramatically as she passed. She didn't seem to have a date, either.

"Then again . . ." Scott rubbed his chin. "The night does have some possibilities. And there's still plenty of time." He grinned and sat down.

"Oh, man," Tommy D. said, picking up a *Bayside Beacon* that someone had left on the table. "What is this doing here? I thought I had finally escaped from it!"

"Someone on the decorating committee must have been reading it," Lindsay said, smiling. "People really seem to like it!"

Tommy turned to the sports page and looked over his soccer article. "It sounds pretty good," he said, rereading it. "People came up to me today and told me they liked it a lot. Thanks to you, babe," he said to Lindsay.

118

"I just fixed it up a little, Tommy D.," Lindsay said, smiling at him.

"Hey Scott, where did the horoscopes go?" Vicki asked teasingly. Scott blushed and grimaced, obviously embarrassed.

"I thought it would be a good idea for me to get out of the prediction business, before I get myself into even more trouble." He shook his head and turned to Lindsay. "I hope you can find someone else to do it," he said apologetically.

"It's not up to me anymore," Lindsay said.

"What do you mean?" Megan asked.

"I'm giving up my job as editor in chief," Lindsay announced.

"You're *what*?" Tommy said.

Everyone started talking at once, objecting to Lindsay's decision. Lindsay held up her hands to silence them.

"My mind is made up," she said firmly. "Editor in chief is definitely a job for a junior or senior. I'm just going to write the occasional article—no muss, no fuss."

"Yo, that's okay by me," Tommy said. "You were getting really strung out over the paper."

"Actually, I know what you mean," Megan said.

"Working for the school newspaper was a huge commitment—and I only wrote two tiny articles."

"Yeah. The stress gave me eczema!" Vicki said, scratching her forearm.

"Hey, don't scratch your flakes on me, Vicki," Weasel said, mixing the papaya punch with grape juice and cola. "Mmm, delicious!" he said, offering some to Manya. She sipped it and smiled at him, delighted.

"Is delicious!" she agreed.

"Well, guys," Scott said, "I propose a toast."

"Ooooh," the girls said, all together.

"No, seriously!" Scott raised his glass of punch. The others raised theirs, too.

"Here's to the *Beacon*," Scott announced. "And freedom from it!"

Everybody toasted and cheered.